THE LOST PRINCE

PEGGY DOWNING

Illustrated by
Sherry Neidigh

A Sequel to *Brill of Exitorn*

Original title:

Segra and Stargull

Bob Jones University Press, Greenville, South Carolina 29614

Library of Congress Cataloging-in-Publication Data

Downing, Peggy, 1924–
   [Segra and Stargull]
   The lost prince / Peggy Downing.
      p.   cm. — (Pennant)
   "Original title: Segra and Stargull."
   "A sequel to Brill of Exitorn."
   Summary: As they set out on a dangerous journey, Segra to find
her parents and Brill to search for the lost prince of Exitorn, the two
friends are helped in their quest by a beautiful meladora bird named
Stargull.
   ISBN 0-89084-834-3
   [1. Fantasy.   2. Christian life—Fiction.]   I. Title.
II. Series.
PZ7.D75935Lo   1995
[Fic]—dc20   95–19932
                                            CIP
                                            AC

The Lost Prince

Edited by Michelle Pryde

© 1987 Peggy Downing
© 1995 Bob Jones University Press
Greenville, South Carolina 29614

ISBN 0-89084-834-3

15   14   13   12   11   10   9   8   7   6   5   4   3   2   1

For my Critique Group:
Wonda Layton, Diana Kruger,
Joan Biggar, Kathy Alderman,
Carol Christiansen, and 'Leen Pollinger

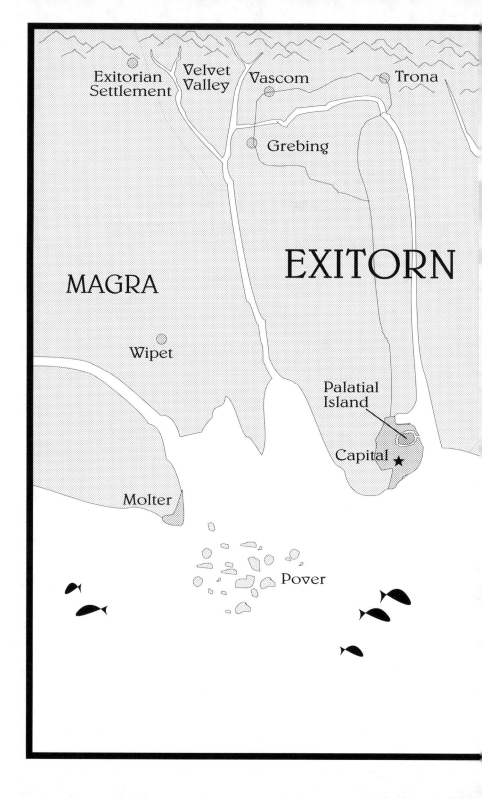

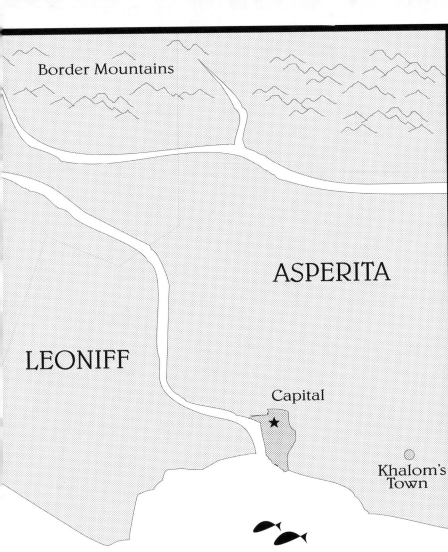

Border Mountains

ASPERITA

LEONIFF

Capital

★

Khalom's
Town

Contents

1

Brill's Promise

Segra grabbed Brill's arm as their wooden cart rattled out of the forest. "Look!" She pointed to the jagged, snow-tipped mountains that rose beyond the fields of Grebing. "Those are the Border Mountains."

Brill smiled. "See, you are not too far from home." His father reined in the horse, and they clattered to a stop in front of a small stone cottage.

Brill leaped to the ground, followed by his father. The door of the cottage flew open, and a woman ran toward them, arms outstretched.

Segra climbed down from the cart too, but she did not follow Brill. She tried not to watch the joyous reunion. It had been a long trip from the king's palace to this little village, and she still was not home yet.

She studied the sheep grazing on the hills beyond the cottage. In the distance, the Border Mountains stood waiting. She sighed.

Two years ago, Emperor Immane had seized her, forcing her to serve as companion to Princess Florette. In spite of Florette's kindness, life at the palace had been filled with danger.

Brill's mother was still talking to her husband. "I can hardly believe that you are here, Stronall."

"Ah, Calda, I feared I would never see you again." He held her close. "I would have come if I could, but Emperor Immane did not permit palace workers to go home. I missed you every day."

"I missed you too," said Brill.

His mother put an arm around him and smoothed his brown hair. "You have grown so tall."

He smiled, holding his shoulders very straight. "I am almost thirteen. Come, Mother." He led her toward Segra. "Come and meet Segra, my good friend. Her parents live somewhere in the Border Mountains."

Brill's mother took Segra's hand. "Welcome, my child. You may stay with us for as long as you wish."

Segra curtsied. "Thank you, madam."

She followed Brill's mother into the one-room cottage. A fire burned in a large stone fireplace, and a wooden table and four chairs stood in one corner. Segra stepped over to the fire, welcoming its heat.

After Brill had taken care of the horses, he joined her at the fireplace. "I have promised to help Segra find her parents," he said.

His mother turned to him with a worried face. "The road leading to the mountains is not safe, my son. I have heard many tales about robbers."

"I think robbers usually look for rich people," said Brill.

His father nodded. "Brill is right. Robbers would not expect Brill and Segra to have anything of value."

Warmed now, Segra took off her cloak. She could not help looking down at the blue dress she wore. It was wrinkled and stained, but the rubies and other jewels on its skirt gleamed as brightly as ever.

Both of Brill's parents were staring at it.

Quickly she explained. "I am still wearing the dress that Princess Florette gave me." She paused, thinking about the robbers. "Perhaps I should cut off the jewels and put them in a pouch to wear under my clothes."

"A wise plan, my child," said Brill's mother. "I will help you." She turned to her husband. "Do you have any news about my father?"

He put a comforting arm around his wife. "It is sad news, my dear. That wicked emperor had Father thrown to the dinogators. We tried to rescue him, but the fall broke several of his bones. He died in my arms."

"I feared as much." Her voice trembled. "So much joy and so much sorrow all in one day." She wiped her eyes.

"Your father would want us to think about the joy," said her husband. He leaned over the fire, adding more branches. "Father died bravely, knowing he had done his best to help others in his lifetime."

Brill's mother nodded. Silently she picked up a bowl of purple roots and put it on the table.

Brill looked up from his seat by the fire. "I wish Grandfather could be here to see that life is much better for everyone—now that King Talder is ruling Exitorn again."

"But the king is old," his father said. "I hope he can find his lost son so there will be someone to rule when he dies."

"What happened to Prince Silgar?" asked Brill's mother. She was slicing the purple roots and dropping them into the stew pot that hung over the fire.

"He disguised himself as a peasant and went to live in the countryside so he would learn about the people's problems," answered Brill's father. "He was going to return to the palace after three years, but by then Immane had taken over. No one has heard from the prince. Even King Talder does not know what happened to him."

"If he is alive, surely he will return, now that his father is king again," said Brill's mother.

"But does he know about the revolution?" asked Brill.

"When Immane took over, I imagine the prince found a good place to hide," Brill's father said. "It is possible he has not heard what happened."

Brill looked at Segra hopefully. "He may be hiding somewhere in the Border Mountains where your parents are. When I take you home, I am going to look for him."

"There are lots of caves and hidden valleys in the mountains," Segra answered.

Brill's mother shook her head. "Son, I think you have had enough adventures for a while." She took a loaf of black bread from the shelf above the table. Then she added slowly, "But I know it is important to find the lost prince."

Her husband nodded. "Yes, it is. We are proud of you, son; you have served your country well. I would go with you if I did not have so many responsibilities here."

"I have an idea," Segra said. "Now that King Talder has started the messenger service again, I will write to Father and ask him to come and get me."

Brill smiled. "That is a good plan. But I still want to go to the mountains to look for the lost prince."

Segra nodded. "We can both look. Father will help us."

After they had eaten, Segra curled up for a nap, but Brill started for the door. "There is one thing I have been wanting to do ever since I got here. I am going up in the hills to find Curly." He turned to Segra. "I will bring him down so you can pet him."

His mother smiled up at him. "Curly is no longer a lamb. He is just one of the flock now."

"He will know me," said Brill confidently.

But he was gone for a long time, and he returned looking downcast. "I called and called, but none of the sheep came to me. Finally I found a sheep with markings like Curly's. I petted him and talked to him, but he did not rub up against me. He must have forgotten me."

"You could find a new lamb for a pet," said his mother, but Brill only sighed. He walked slowly out of the cottage, and Segra knew that he wanted to be alone with his disappointment.

The next day Brill's mother gave Segra a quill pen, ink, and a square of rough paper so she could write to her parents.

Dear Father and Mother,

I am staying at a farm near Grebing with my friend Brill. He was Emprince Grossder's companion. You have probably heard that King Talder has overthrown the wicked Immane. Brill and I helped the king escape from prison, but they caught us and threw us to the dinogators in the castle moat. We found out that dinogators do not usually harm people. I even made friends with one named Peachy. I am sure he understands when I talk to him.

I have much to tell you—about the caverns under Palatial Island and how we helped to restore the rightful king to Exitorn, but most of all I just want to see you! Could you come to Grebing to get me? I miss you so much.

Love, Segra

After she had sent the letter, Segra waited impatiently. Surely Father would come within a week. Or he would send a note. But nothing happened, and after ten long days, she decided that her letter must have been lost.

"I cannot wait any longer," she said to Brill. "I must go home." Brill looked thoughtful for a moment, then he declared, "I will go with you as we originally planned."

"Oh, Brill, I hate to take you away from home. Your mother will be so sad to see you go."

"I will miss her too, but Mother and Father agree that you cannot go alone." His eyes lit up with enthusiasm. "We could leave tomorrow."

It was early the next morning when Segra awoke. Silently she stood up, pulled her cloak around her dress, and tiptoed toward the door. She stepped out to watch the sunrise gild the snowcapped mountain peaks. Home! Brill's father had said they might be able to walk to the mountains in one day. Was it possible that by tonight she would actually be home?

Brill joined her outside, and she exclaimed, "I can hardly believe I am so close to getting home."

He nodded. "I know you are excited. But we have a long walk ahead of us. It is too bad we cannot use the horses and cart that King Talder gave Father."

"Yes," said Segra. "But paying the debts on your farm is more important, so I understand why your father had to sell them."

"We will manage," Brill said with a smile, and he left to finish the chores. Segra went inside to help Brill's mother pick up the straw mattresses and tidy the cottage.

When Brill and his father came in from the barn, everyone sat down at the rough wooden table to eat porridge. "I packed you both some lunch," Brill's mother said. "Bread, cheese, and berriballs."

"Oh, thank you," said Segra.

Brill smiled at his mother. "Many times, back at the palace, I wished for a taste of your bread," he said. "I am glad we can take some with us."

"Be sure to take your fire stones too," she said. "At least you can always get a fire going to keep warm."

As soon as breakfast was over, Segra took her ivory comb, a bit of soap, and a towel, and she tied them into her kerchief. She pinned the sack of jewels to her underdress and tucked in the ends of the gold cord at her waist. Most of the gold had worn off, but she remembered how shiny the belt had been when Florette had given her the beautiful blue dress. She smoothed the blue fabric regretfully. She had washed it, but the stains from the filthy dungeon and the moat would not come out. Perhaps Mother would make her some new clothes.

"I am ready to go," she said.

"It is time," agreed Brill. He stuffed his fire stones, his knife, and their lunch into the sack he wore on his belt. Then he filled a goatskin with water and tied it to his belt. "I think I will take my bow and a few arrows too."

"You have quite an assortment hanging on your belt," Segra said.

"Yes—so I am prepared for whatever may happen." He hugged his mother and father. "Do not worry if I do not return right away. First I will make sure Segra gets home safely. After that, it may take me a long time to find the prince."

"We understand," said his father.

"Be careful," added his mother.

"I will," he promised.

Segra curtsied to Brill's mother. "Thank you for your kindness, madam."

The road to the mountains led through Grebing, then curved down toward the river. At the river, Segra cried, "Look, there is a dinogator!"

"Maybe it is our friend Peachy."

Segra called out a greeting, but the long, scaly body did not stir. The creature did not even open its eyes.

"If that was Peachy, he would swim over to us," declared Segra. "Oh, well, I am glad the dinogators are free again to swim in the rivers instead of being kept in that moat around Palatial Island."

They crossed the river and entered deep woods where tall evergreens blotted out the sun. Segra shivered and walked faster, watching for robbers who might be hiding behind trees.

She was glad when they reached the end of the woods. The road ran on through farmland with plowed fields, orchards, and pastures.

"Are you hungry?" asked Brill.

Segra checked the sun. "It is not noon yet."

"I know, but I am hungry enough to eat a dinogator."

They found a grassy mound in a pasture, and Brill opened the sack fastened to his belt. He handed Segra a piece of bread, then cut them each a slice of cheese. As Segra bit into the bread, she realized how hungry she was.

"We had better save some of this for supper tonight," Brill said, "—in case we cannot find your parents right away."

"We will find them. I just know we will," Segra said. "We are getting closer to the Border Mountains." She jumped to her feet, unable to rest any longer.

Brill pulled out the map his father had drawn for him. "We should be coming to the town of Vascom next. That is about halfway."

They trudged on, passing through Vascom and into farmland again. Ahead of them rose forested foothills, and soon the road led through deep woods.

They had not gone far into the forest when they heard screams. "Someone is in trouble," Segra cried. She darted forward. Brill grabbed her cloak.

"Wait. And be quiet," he whispered. "Let us slip through the trees to see what is happening. If there are robbers, we do not want them to see us."

Segra nodded. Brill led the way into the thick underbrush. He picked up a stout stick and pushed aside the vines and bushes that barred their way.

"Help! Help!" came frenzied shouts.

Segra pulled her dress loose from a thorny vine. "This is taking too long."

"Shhh," warned Brill. "We are getting close."

They peered between the bushes. Two men bent over a young boy, beating him. "Your money!" one of them barked. He knocked the boy to the ground. The other man jerked a money sack from the boy's belt and kicked him.

Brill put an arrow into his bow and shot it, then another. *Thwack! Thwack!* Both arrows lodged in a tree above the robbers' heads.

They looked up in alarm. "Who is shooting at us?" one of them cried. "Let us be gone!"

Brill waited for another minute, then stepped out of the woods into the clearing. The boy on the ground groaned in pain. Segra took a handful of leaves and wiped the blood from the boy's face.

"Who are you?" he moaned.

"Friends. We want to help," answered Segra. "Where does it hurt the most?"

"All over."

"Are any bones broken?"

"All of them."

"No, no, I do not think so." Segra felt his legs, then his arms. "I do not feel any broken bones. Can you stand?"

"I would rather stay here and die," the boy whispered.

Brill took his arms and helped him sit up.

The boy shook his head. "Do not bother with me. There is nothing you can do."

Brill shot a glance at Segra and raised his eyebrows.

"If we had not come by, they might have killed you," she said. What was the matter with him?

"I wish they had," he muttered. "My master sent me to Vascom to sell a goat. When I return with no money, he will beat me."

"But you could not help being robbed," said Segra. "He will see that you are hurt."

"He is a stingy man with a terrible temper. I cannot face him without that money."

Segra looked at Brill. "Perhaps you could help him to walk a little." She stepped back into the bushes and reached for the sack of jewels pinned to her underdress. She pulled out a ruby and returned while the boy was taking a few steps on his own. "Give this to your master," she said with a smile.

He stared at the glittering red jewel. "Where did you get it?"

"Never mind. I am giving it to you."

"I think this is worth more than a goat."

"Quite likely. Your master will be pleased."

He felt his face. "Am I still bleeding?"

"Only a little," said Segra.

For the first time, he smiled. "I am still sore, but I am no longer afraid to go back to my master. Thank you."

He limped through the trees with Brill and Segra beside him. "Do not tell anyone where you got the ruby," said Brill.

"Well—all right, if you do not want me to. But I am going to show it to my friends before I give it to my master." He opened his hand to stare at the ruby again. "I have never held a jewel before."

They left the boy in the next village, and when they were alone again, Brill said, "I know we had to help him, but I am afraid of what is going to happen."

"You think he will tell?"

"I am certain he will tell his friends that he was beaten and a girl gave him a ruby. News spreads fast in a village. Every robber around here will be looking for the girl who hands out jewels."

2
Disappointment

Segra looked behind her uneasily, but the road was empty. How soon would some greedy person set out to catch them?

"Let us run," Brill said. "The farther away we get, the safer we will be."

They ran through the level farmland until they came to a hill. Soon Segra began to pant. "Nobody is following us," she gasped.

"We still need to hurry to Trona," Brill said, but he slowed to a walk.

"The Book of Wisdom says something about jewels." Segra frowned, trying to remember. "Oh, yes, I think it says, *As we share our jewels with others, we will receive blessings beyond the value of earthly treasure.*"

Brill nodded. "My grandfather used to quote that. He said the proverb does not mean real jewels. It means we should share with one another, and if we all share, the world will be a happier place. But most people do not live by that rule."

"I know." Segra tried to ignore the ache in her legs. I hope no one tries to rob us, she thought. Nothing must keep me from getting back home.

Late that afternoon, they heard a rumbling noise as they trudged up another hill.

"What is that?" asked Segra. They hurried to the top of the hill where they could see the road ahead. A long column of soldiers in green uniforms was marching toward Trona.

"Quick," cried Brill. "Let us follow them. Nobody will dare to rob us, not with soldiers on the road."

They followed the soldiers all the way to Trona. The first thing Segra wanted to do was go to the marketplace. Perhaps she would see someone there from her mountain village.

A man stood in front of a cart piled high with carrots and jimger roots. "Fresh vegetables," he shouted. "Buy them here."

In a nearby booth a woman held up a length of gray wool. "Fine quality wool," she called. "Low prices."

Segra scanned the faces of the shoppers. "I hoped to see a familiar face from our mountain settlement, but I do not recognize anyone." She sighed. "Well, I will just have to find out how they are when I get to the valley where we live."

"How long will that take?" asked Brill.

"About two hours."

He looked longingly at a roasting chicken. "I am hungry."

"It would be better not to spend another jewel, and we still have berriballs."

"I know, but I crave a taste of meat."

"I am sure Mother will fix you a fine meal when we get home."

Brill nodded, looking glum. "Let us go. I can climb on an empty stomach if you can."

Segra wanted to say something funny. "I thought I would use my feet," she said with a giggle.

Brill gave her a smile, and they turned toward the mountain.

The trail was steep, winding back and forth among the trees. Finally the evergreens thinned out until only a few windswept trees clung to the rocky hillside. Segra pointed out familiar landmarks. "Look, Brill, there is Mount Snola. Its glaciers never melt, so it is white all year round."

"It reminds me of a big dish of rice pudding."

"We still have the berriballs left," she said. They rested on a flat rock while they ate.

"Are you sure you do not want the last one?" asked Brill.

"You eat it." Segra licked the sweet juice from her fingers. "All I can think about is seeing Father and Mother again." She jumped to her feet and started down the path.

At last they reached the place where a smaller path turned off to the left. Segra smiled. "Our home is just behind the next ridge."

Brill raised an eyebrow. "Looks like a long way."

"It will not take long. We just have to go down this ridge, across the valley, and up the other side. Come on."

Brill sighed. "Be patient, stomach. You will be fed eventually."

They followed the rocky path downward, crossed a creek on steppingstones, and began to climb again. Now the path had disappeared, and some places were so steep that they had to pull themselves up by shrubs or rock outcroppings.

Brill stopped for a moment. "Why did your parents ever choose such a hard place to get to?" he asked.

Segra was glad for a chance to catch her breath. "My father is very independent, and he wanted to be free. Up here, we were not bothered by the emperor's soldiers—the ones who took a share of the crops."

Brill nodded. "We always dreaded the day the gatherers came. If they thought we were not giving them their seventy-five percent, they could take our whole farm."

Segra grew quiet as they climbed over the top of the ridge and turned down toward a broad meadow. The settlement of five cottages below them seemed almost invisible in the folds of the surrounding mountains. She hurried down across the sparse grass to the tiny stone hut she shared with her parents. At the wooden door she paused, taking a deep breath. She pulled it open and stepped inside.

No one was there. "Where are they?" she exclaimed. She stared into the gloom. "What about my letter?" There it was, on the floor. The messenger had pushed it under the door, but no one had been there to get it.

Slowly she bent and picked it up. "The seal has not been broken. They have not even seen my letter. Where could they be?"

"We will find them," said Brill.

Segra walked to the food cupboards. They were bare. She trailed a finger through the layer of dust that had settled on everything. "No one has lived here for a long time," she said in a choked voice.

Brill's calm voice steadied her. "Let us go talk to your neighbors."

Segra nodded, fighting back her tears. She followed him outside and turned toward a cottage with smoke rising from its chimney. At her knock, a gray-haired man opened the door.

She tried to smile as the man squinted at her. "Segra?" he asked. "Are you really little Segra—alive and well?"

She nodded. "Yes, Balt. This is my friend Brill. Can you tell me where Father and Mother are?"

"Come in, children. Welcome to our cottage."

They stepped inside. The back of the cottage extended into a cave, and it was dark, except for an oil lamp and a fire at the back which gave flickering light. The aroma of cooking meat filled the air. Balt spoke to an old woman, who sat by the fireplace. "Eila, do you remember Segra? She has come back to visit us."

Eila grasped her hand. "Let me look at you. Why, you have become a young lady! How wonderful to see you again."

"I am glad to be back," Segra said. "But no one is at home. Do you know where I can find my parents?"

"They left here to go to the capital city," Balt said. "We had heard that the emperor was going to throw you to the dinogators. I have never seen Garsil in such anguish. He was determined to find a way to rescue you."

"Did Mother go too?"

"Oh, yes. She suffered her grief more quietly, and she worried that Garsil would run into serious trouble."

Eila smiled. "You must have escaped from the dinogators."

"We were surprised to find that they are friendly—" Brill began.

"But I cannot understand why my parents have not returned," Segra interrupted.

Eila frowned. "Perhaps they decided to stay in the capital. They were planning to visit your mother's sister."

"That would be Aunt Hara," Segra murmured. "I have never met her."

"Your aunt may know where they are," said Balt.

Segra looked at Brill. "I am going to the capital to talk to my aunt," she said firmly.

"All that way?" asked Brill.

"It is my only hope of finding Mother and Father. But I know you want to keep looking for the prince. I will be all right."

Eila rose slowly to her feet. "I have a stew cooking. Share it with us and stay overnight. Perhaps in the morning you can decide what to do."

Before long they were eating the thick hot stew from wooden bowls. Eila passed around a plate of black bread, and Segra thought that it tasted as good as her mother's.

While they ate, Balt said, "I am taking care of your father's goats. I am sure he would not abandon his herd. Why not wait for them here?"

Segra shook her head. "It has been too long. I must find them as soon as I can."

After supper Segra and Brill went outside to watch the sun set behind the jagged range of mountains to the west.

"I am sorry your parents were not here," said Brill.

"I was so sure I would find them." Segra blinked back tears, and all the colors of the sunset ran together.

Brill said, "You would be safer if you waited for your parents here. Balt thinks they will come back."

Segra stared at the green pastures scattered among the rocks of the mountain. She thought of all the times she had waited for her father to return with his goats at sunset. She said, "Something must have happened to them, or they would have returned. I must talk to my aunt."

"What if she says your parents went home?"

"Then I will come back here. Do not worry about me, Brill. I will be all right."

"I am going with you. I promised I would help you find your parents, and I will not leave until we find them."

She wanted to remind him again about the lost prince, but she could not find the words. "I thank you, Brill. Perhaps it will be soon."

The color faded from the sky, and they walked back toward Balt's cottage. Brill must have been thinking about the prince, though, for he said, "Maybe your father will help us search for Prince Silgar."

"I am sure he will—if the prince is still missing. King Talder must have sent men to find him."

Brill nodded. "We will ask for news when we get to the capital."

Eila gave them straw mats to sleep on, and it was warm beside the fire, but for long hours Segra lay awake. What could have happened to Father and Mother? A smoky smell hung in the air, mingled with the smell of the oil lamp and the stew from supper. She fell asleep remembering the good goat-meat stew her mother made.

The next morning when Segra thanked the old couple for their kindness, Eila handed her a packet of food. "Your parents are fine people, and your father has helped many people. He is a wonderful doctor," Eila said. "We want them to come back too. I hope you find them soon."

Brill set a fast pace, and by afternoon they had passed Trona and turned onto the road that led to Exitorn's capital.

"The only time I traveled this road was when soldiers took me to the palace to be a companion to Florette." Segra frowned, remembering.

"Were you as unhappy as I was to be taken to the palace?"

Segra nodded. "I tried not to cry. They would not even let me go up the mountain to say good-bye to my parents." Her voice broke. "I want to see them so much."

When Brill spoke again, his voice was low. "Do not look now, but someone is following us."

"Are you certain?"

"No. Maybe he is just going the same way we are. He left Trona just after we did. I wonder if he could have heard about your jewels."

Segra walked faster. "What should we do?"

"I think we should leave the road. If he does not follow us, we will know he has no evil intentions."

Segra looked across the flat meadowland. "There are no woods to hide in."

"Let us cross the pasture and head for the river. If he keeps coming, we can swim across."

Segra took a quick look behind her. "He looks so strong—I do not think a river is going to stop him."

"Do you have a better plan?"

"No." She wished she had picked up a stout stick.

They hurried across the pasture, and Segra glanced ahead, hoping to find someone to help—maybe a farmer. But there was no one, only a cow chewing its cud.

She looked over her shoulder again. "He is following us."

Brill broke into a run. "Hurry!"

"Stop!" shouted the man. "I want to talk to you!"

Segra ran faster, trying to keep up with Brill. "He is getting closer," she gasped.

"Here is the river." Brill plunged down a steep bank. He stumbled, then cried out in pain and landed on the rocky beach below.

Segra climbed down more carefully and knelt beside him. "Brill, what happened?"

He clenched his fists. "Caught my foot on a tree root. You had better swim across the river—before he gets here."

"I will not leave you. Where does it hurt?"

"My ankle. Run, Segra! He is at the top of the bank!" Brill struggled to his knees and began fitting an arrow into his bow. But before he could take aim, the man jumped down the bank, picked up a rock, and threw it. It splintered Brill's bow, knocking it from his hands.

"Brill, did he hurt you?"

"No. Get away, Segra. Please."

The man started across the rocky beach.

Segra stood up and glared at him. "My friend is hurt. Why are you chasing us?"

He said, "You will not come to any harm, little lady—as long as you give me all your jewels."

"What jewels?"

The man leaped toward her and grabbed her arm.

Segra squirmed, but he held her tight with his powerful hand. "Help! Oh, help!" she screamed.

Brill grabbed the attacker's leg, but he shook him off. Without releasing Segra, the man picked up Brill and flung him into the river.

Segra pulled with all her strength, kicking at the man's leg, trying to twist free from his grip.

"None of that," he snarled, "or I will break your arm." He clamped one arm around her waist. "Where is your money pouch? Ah, here it is."

Segra groaned. If she gave up the jewels, they would have no money for their trip. But she had no other choice.

3
Aunt Hara's News

Segra struggled, gasping for breath. She could hear Brill shouting, "Hurry, hurry!" Who was he calling?

"Are you going to give me that pouch, or do I have to cut your dress to get it?" snarled her attacker.

The man pulled a knife from his belt, then stopped. A terrible noise filled the air.

Segra recognized the angry bellow of a dinogator. Looking toward the river, she saw a dinogator swimming rapidly toward shore. Segra tried to twist away from the man, but he held her tightly as he stared at the creature.

The dinogator growled as it marched up on the beach, showing its long, pointed teeth. It lifted a clawed foot to strike the man, and he pushed Segra forward. The creature quickly reached out a foreleg to stop Segra from falling. The robber turned, scrambled up the bank, and disappeared from sight.

Segra stared at the dinogator's foreleg, noticing that it was crooked. Could this be Peachy? Yes! She hugged the scaly head. "Peachy! You have saved our lives."

Brill limped out of the water. "Are you sure this is Peachy? Dinogators all look alike to me."

"I recognize the spot where I set his broken leg. It did not mend quite straight."

Segra sat down, and Peachy nuzzled her shoulder. "I am sorry I do not have any peaches," she told him. She pulled an apple from Eila's sack of food. Peachy crunched it, giving a deep grunt of satisfaction.

Brill sat beside them, rubbing his ankle.

"Do you think the robber will hide near the road and wait for us?" asked Segra.

"Hard to tell."

"He sure ran away in a hurry." She patted Peachy. "We owe so much to you." She looked at Brill. "The side of your face is bleeding. Did you get hurt when he threw you into the river?"

Brill drew a hand across his face and frowned at the blood on it. "I landed on some rocks sticking up in the water, but I did not know I was bleeding. The scratches do not hurt much."

"How is your ankle?"

"That is my worst problem. It hurts when I put my weight on it, but it is not broken. Are you all right?"

"Yes, now that the robber is gone. I am glad I still have the jewels." Segra put a hand on her skirt. "Perhaps you should ride across the river on Peachy? We can set up camp there until you are able to walk."

Brill nodded. "Good idea. If the robber comes back to look for us here, he will think Peachy ate us." He glanced up at the sky. "Those dark clouds mean rain."

Segra patted Peachy. "I know you do not mind rain, but Brill needs shelter so his clothes will dry. Maybe we can find a tree to camp under." She turned to Brill. "Peachy really does understand me. You will see."

Peachy slipped back to the water, and Brill climbed onto his back for the ride across. When Peachy returned for Segra, she took off her shoes and tucked up her long skirt so it would not get wet. Brill waved and shouted at them, pointing downstream, and Peachy swam a short way down the river. The dinogator stopped in front of a log hut that had only two walls standing. Other logs lay on the ground, and the thatched roof looked as if it were ready to slide off. Brill limped down to join them, and he crawled into the only sheltered corner of the hut as the first raindrops began to fall.

"Thank you, Peachy," Segra said. "This will do fine." She crouched beside Brill, watching as the rain turned into a heavy downpour. Peachy lay down outside the shack, as if he enjoyed the shower.

Segra bent to look at Brill's ankle. "It is swelling. After the rain stops, I will bind it tightly, but you still will not be able to walk tomorrow." Gently she touched his cheek. "How does your face feel?"

"A little sore, but a face does not have to do much—except eat and talk."

"Do not forget seeing and breathing," she said. "Thank you for trying to save me from the robber."

"Well, I tried, but Peachy is the one who really saved you." He eyed the bag of food. "Do you think it is supper time?"

While they munched on black bread and goat cheese, Segra said, "We should not eat too much now, for we do not know when we will get more food."

Brill nodded. "I know. I just hope my ankle feels better soon so we can travel again."

That night, Segra slept deeply, knowing Peachy was guarding them. She opened her eyes to sunshine and saw Brill sitting outside the hut. He seemed to be studying the fallen logs. "How is your ankle?" she asked.

"It still hurts some."

"We will have to stay here another day at least," she said. "But by tomorrow you might be able to walk on it. Your face will heal better if I can find some of the herb that my father likes to use. First, I am going to see what I can find for breakfast."

She picked some tart, juicy blackberries from bushes growing beside their shelter. Peachy enjoyed the blackberry bushes too. He crunched them up, the berries, leaves, thorns, and all. Segra brought Brill handful after handful until he had eaten enough.

While he was eating, she found the heart-shaped leaves of the herb she had been looking for and crushed them to bathe his face with.

"Thank you," Brill said when she had finished. "That feels better already." He wiped his berry-stained hands on a leaf. "I have an idea. If we tie those logs together into a raft, we can float down the river to the capital."

Segra frowned. "Are you serious? What will you tie them with?"

"Clinper vines. They are very strong. Grandfather and I used to tie fences together with them."

Segra walked over to inspect a fallen log. Could Brill's idea really work? "The wood still looks in good condition."

"The logs are Herconne wood, which is known for its endurance," Brill said. "The only question is, can we tie them together tightly enough so they will not separate?"

"Where will you find the vines?"

"Clinper vines are everywhere. Are you not familiar with them?"

Segra shook her head.

Brill limped to a patch of weeds growing beside a stump. He pulled out a long strand of reddish vine and cut it with his knife.

"Oh, so that is what they are. I never knew their name," said Segra. "I can gather some while you start the tying."

Brill looped a vine around the first log, then ran the two ends of the vine around the second log, tying it tightly to the first log. He kept tying vines around the logs and to each other until he had five logs fastened securely together.

After Segra had gathered as many vines as Brill needed, she began picking blackberries. Then she pulled up wild jimger roots. They could stay alive on jimger roots if they had to.

"How long will it take to float down the river to the capital?" she asked.

"I do not know."

"I am trying to figure out how much food we will need. I wish I had changed some of my jewels for money so we could buy food from the peddlers on the river."

"There was no place to do that in the small towns we have been through. We will do it in the capital."

"If we are hungry enough, we can chew on jimger roots."

Brill frowned. "I have never eaten them raw, but I know I do not like them cooked."

"We ate them when we first lived in the mountains. They are bitter, but Mother said they were good for us."

Brill sighed. "I can eat them if there is nothing else."

"I also found a spring, so we can fill your goatskin with fresh water," said Segra.

"Good. I want to push our raft to the water's edge this afternoon so we can leave early tomorrow morning."

"How is your ankle?"

"It is sore, but all I have to do once we are underway is sit still and let the river carry us."

Segra frowned. "But what if we run into something?"

"I found a couple of boards. We can steer with them."

Late that afternoon, Brill called Segra over to see the finished raft. "Now all we have to do is get it into the water," he said.

Segra braced her feet, took a deep breath, and pushed. The raft did not budge. Brill bent down to help her. Together they shoved against the heavy logs, but they did not move. Again and again they tried.

Brill sprawled onto the ground, panting. "I should have built it closer to the river. I will have to take it apart and move it a few logs at a time and then retie it all."

"Wait a minute," Segra said. "I have an idea."

She ran to where Peachy was dozing in the shallow water. "Peachy, can you help us move our raft to the river?"

He opened his eyes, grunted, and followed Segra to the raft. First he circled slowly around it, then he lifted one end with his snout and flipped it over. After three more flips, the raft landed at the water's edge.

"I am so glad it did not fall apart," Brill said. He smiled as he put the steering boards and two poles on the raft.

Segra patted Peachy's head. "You are wonderful."

The next morning Peachy pushed the raft into the water, and they climbed aboard. Brill poled them toward deeper water. He showed Segra how to sit on one side of the raft and use a board to control its direction.

The current carried the raft downstream, and the sun warmed them. On the way they passed a few peddlers in rowboats heading for the villages. Peachy swam alongside and exchanged greetings with the dinogators he met. When it grew dark, they beached the raft beside the river and slept.

The next day they rose at dawn to continue their journey. By the third day they could see the castle towers on Palatial Island. Now the river was becoming crowded with sailing ships and many smaller boats.

After they almost ran into a rowboat, Brill said, "We had better walk the rest of the way. We cannot steer well enough to get safely through all these boats." They steered to the side, and he used his pole to push them close to the beach.

Segra hugged Peachy and bade him good-bye. "Thank you, Peachy. You made it all possible."

As they followed a winding road that led into the city, Segra said, "You are not limping much now."

"My ankle feels much better," he said. "Thanks to Peachy, that raft worked out well."

Finally they neared the castle, and they walked along the moat, looking silently across at the stone towers. "It seems like a long time since we lived there," Brill said at last.

Segra nodded. "I wonder if King Talder has found his lost son yet."

"Maybe your aunt will know."

"She lives near the marketplace, I think." Segra led the way to the crowded central square where farmers sold fresh vegetables and fruit. "Florette and I liked exploring the market," she said. "Of course we always had soldiers along because Florette was a princess."

"You were fortunate," Brill said. "Grossder and I never left Palatial Island because he was too fat to move around much."

Brill stopped by a booth where meat chunks cooked over a metal brazier. "That meat smells delicious." Segra could hardly hear his voice above the noise of the merchants calling out their bargains.

Segra nodded in agreement, but she did not slow down. If only they had a few coins, they could buy some meat and a plum tart too. Finally she stopped at a booth where a woman sold wool. "Do you know Hara, the weaver?"

"Everyone knows Hara." The woman pointed. "She lives there—at the fifth door."

Segra and Brill hurried down the street lined with small shops. The fifth door was wide open, and inside a woman sat weaving cloth on a large wooden loom.

"Come in," she called when she saw Brill and Segra at her doorway. "Finest cloth in the city at fair prices. What do you need?"

Segra asked, "Are you Hara, sister of Nalane?"

"Yes. How do you know Nalane?"

"She is my mother. I am Segra."

Hara's plump face shone with a bright smile. "What a wonderful surprise." She jumped up and threw her arms around Segra. "How can this be? We thought you were dead. But yes—you have my sister's blond hair and deep blue eyes."

"You thought I was dead?" asked Segra in amazement. "Is that what my parents think too?"

Hara sighed. "Yes, my dear, I am afraid so. Unfortunately, they arrived here on Empire Day. They had heard that you were to be executed. Garsil was determined to approach the emperor, to beg for your life, but he was not even permitted to set foot on Palatial Island."

"Oh, how terrible for them! Poor Father and Mother!" Segra cried. "If only they could have known what really happened. I must find them."

"They left the next day to go to the country of Magra. Garsil said he could no longer bear to live in this country."

Magra? Segra blinked back tears. How could she ever find her parents?

"If they had stayed a few more days," Brill said, "they could have seen Emperor Immane replaced by good King Talder."

Hara nodded at him from her loom. "I told Garsil that I had heard there would be an uprising against Immane, but he insisted on leaving immediately."

"I must go to Magra to find them," said Segra.

Brill frowned. "Have you heard any news about the crown prince?"

"No, there has been no word of him," Aunt Hara said. "The people are worried because there is no heir to the throne. If King Talder died, there could be a war to decide who should rule." She stood up and put an arm around Segra. "Come, my dears. You are both looking pale and thin. You must have a good meal and tell me how you escaped the dinogators."

Segra smiled at her, and Brill spoke quickly. "Thank you very much!"

Aunt Hara led them to a small room in the back of her shop. Chicken soup simmered in a black pot hanging over the fireplace, filling the air with a tantalizing aroma. Aunt Hara ladled the soup into pewter bowls and put a large loaf of bread on the table, along with butter and honey.

For a few minutes, they ate in silence. Then, while Brill was buttering his fourth slice of bread, Segra asked her aunt, "Where can I find a ship to Magra?"

"If you go down to the docks, someone will point one out. The weavers do quite a bit of trade with Magra, even though King Gabron is a dishonest man." Aunt Hara sliced more bread with quick, angry strokes. "Last year he took a big shipment of wool cloth, then he tried to cheat us by only paying half of the agreed price. I do not trust him."

"Why did Father and Mother go there?" asked Segra.

Her aunt shrugged. "It is nearby. Many people from Exitorn who hated or feared the emperor have settled in Magra." She pushed the bread plate closer to Brill, then asked, "Do you have money to pay for your fare?"

"I have some jewels that Princess Florette gave me," said Segra.

"You had better exchange them for coins before you buy passage on the ship," advised Aunt Hara. "I shall come along to make sure that you get a fair price."

After lunch Segra and Brill went with her to a jeweler, and he exchanged two of Segra's emeralds for silver coins.

Then they bade Aunt Hara farewell and walked down to the docks. "Do you know of any ships going to Magra?" Segra asked an old seaman.

He pointed to a wooden ship with a single mast. "That'un there is leaving at high tide," he said.

Segra approached a man who was loading bundles onto the ship. "How much does it cost to go to Magra?"

"Half fare for such a pretty maid," he answered.

"I am going too," said Brill.

"Well now, for an ugly fellow like you, it will cost twice as much." The man chuckled. "Three tencoins for the pair of you."

"When do we sail?" asked Segra.

"At dawn. You had better board tonight."

"How long does the trip take?" asked Segra.

"About three days if the wind is with us."

Brill turned to Segra. "I must send a message to my parents."

"Yes, we can stop at the messenger station on our way to the marketplace. We need food for our journey." Segra took one last look at the ship. "Do you think it will get us there?"

Brill shrugged. "It looks rather small to go through ocean waves, but it is old, so it must have survived for many years."

"Brill, you do not have to go," Segra said suddenly. "I will be all right on the ship."

"I promised I would help you find your parents, and I will keep my promise." Brill wore a determined expression.

"But I do not want to trouble you."

He smiled. "Segra, you have complicated my life since I first met you. I do not know why I keep tagging after you except I am afraid that, without me, you would never survive."

She tossed her head. "I thought we were friends."

"We are, and it usually takes two of us to get out of the predicaments you get us in, does it not?"

Segra laughed. "Well, yes, I have to admit that sometimes you have been very helpful. I am glad you are coming with me."

4
Tossing Waves

That evening, Brill and Segra ate supper beside the castle moat. Segra watched the people coming and going from Palatial Island. Citizens of Exitorn were now permitted to cross the drawbridge and see the king, stroll in the gardens, or enjoy the play park.

"It might be fun to live in the palace now that King Talder is the ruler," she said, "but what I want most is to be with my parents again."

Brill skipped a stone across the water. "I wish we had time to visit King Talder."

"We will do that when we come back." Segra looked at her dress, more tattered than ever after their journey to the capital. "I will need a new dress before I see the king."

"King Talder is not impressed by jewels and riches like Emperor Immane was."

Segra sighed. "The Book of Wisdom says, *Goodness in the heart is worth much more than rich raiment on the body.* Still, I do not like to look shabby."

After they had finished eating, Brill stood. "The sun is getting low. We had better board our ship."

As they walked toward the docks, Brill said, "I have been thinking. Maybe the prince fled to Magra when Immane began to rule."

Segra nodded. "Aunt Hara told us that many Exitornians escaped from Immane by going to other countries."

"The prince knew Immane would imprison him or even kill him."

"But he might have gone to Leoniff or Asperita."

"Perhaps." Brill fell silent for a long time. Then he added, "But when we get to Magra, I am going to ask if anyone has seen him."

The dock was a noisy place, with men shouting to one another as they loaded cargo onto many ships. Brill and Segra found their ship, but they had to wait while men loaded it with sacks of barley. When the loading was finished, they went aboard, and Brill paid their fare with money Segra had given him for that purpose.

The first mate took the money and nodded toward a hole with a ladder leading below. "You can find a spot in the hold or stay on deck. You are the only passengers on this trip, so you have your choice."

"Which is better?" asked Segra.

"Depends on what you like. The deck is cold, but you are not so apt to get seasick in the open air. Below deck it is dark and smelly, but you will be protected from rain," said the mate.

"I vote for the deck," said Brill, and Segra nodded in agreement.

A small boy ran up to the mate. "Uncle Iba, can I help you put up the sail tomorrow morning?" he cried.

"No, that is man's work, Lopet," his uncle said. "You are not strong enough yet." The boy looked disappointed, but he did not make a fuss. Segra thought he looked like a puppy at the heels of its master as he followed his uncle all over the ship.

She and Brill explored the deck, looking for a sleeping spot. Segra pointed to a place that was protected from the north wind by the captain's cabin. "How about this?"

"Looks good," Brill said. "The sky is clear, so we should not have to worry about rain tonight."

As soon as they sat down on the deck, Lopet walked over to gaze at them with curious, brown eyes.

"Do you live onboard the ship?" asked Brill.

"No, I am on a trip with Uncle Iba," answered Lopet in his high-pitched voice. "I am a good helper."

"How old are you?" asked Segra.

"Almost eight. I live with Papa and Mama in Magra, but when I grow bigger, I am going to sea." Lopet pointed to a man heading below. "That is the cook's helper. He may need my help in the galley. I cannot talk longer." He scurried away.

Brill grinned. "He will be a good sailor some-day."

As darkness fell, Segra and Brill watched the bright stars gleaming in the moonless sky. Segra's eyes grew heavy, and she curled up on the wooden deck, pulling her cloak over herself. She soon fell asleep, rocked by the gentle swells of the harbor waves.

The next morning, the sailors set to work early. Segra watched with fascination as they hoisted the big white mainsail on the tall mast. She leaned on the ship's rail, letting the brisk wind blow her hair into tangles. Perhaps the wind would blow the ship to Magra quickly so she could find her parents.

Brill pointed to the stern. "The helmsman is steering the ship with the tiller."

"It works better than our boards on the raft."

"We got down the river without crashing into anything."

The first mate strode past, and two paces behind him marched little Lopet. Segra nudged Brill. "See that little boy? I am afraid someone will step on him—he keeps getting in the way. Perhaps you could talk to him for a while?"

"Sure," agreed Brill. "Hey, Lopet, want to hear a riddle?" Lopet ran over to them.

"What is bigger than a boat and always wears a wet coat?"

"I do not know."

"Sure you do. Think, Lopet, think."

"If it is always wet, it must live in the sea. I know, a whale." He jumped up and down in excitement.

"You are smart, Lopet," said Segra.

"Ask me another."

"What has scales, but they are not for weighing?"

"That is easy—a fish."

Brill entertained Lopet until they had left the harbor. His uncle stopped by to explain. "Now we will head for open sea. A large ship cannot sail across the bay between Magra and Exitorn because of rocks and shallow water. We have to go beyond the islands and approach Magra from the sea."

"Someday I will have my own ship, and I will sail to the end of the world," declared Lopet.

"Do not go too far, or you will fall off the edge," warned Brill.

"I would not fall off," said Lopet. "I am going to sail to the edge and look over to see what is below."

Segra laughed. "Lopet, when you do that, come back and tell me what you see."

Iba pointed to starboard. "You can see some islands now."

"There are so many!" said Segra.

"Over thirty," said Iba, "if you count the small rocky ones with only a few trees."

Brill asked, "Is Pover one of these islands?"

"Pover is an outer island. We will be passing close to it early tomorrow. Maybe Emperor Immane will wave to us. That is where he was sent after the revolution."

"Have you ever seen him?" asked Brill.

"No, but I wonder about him. It must have been a shock to be sent away to a primitive island with no servants," said Iba.

"He has his family with him," said Segra.

"Yes, but they are not used to working either. I wonder what he does all day on that little island. I certainly would not want to trade places with him." Iba chuckled and left to resume his duties.

"I wish I could stop to see Florette," Segra said.

Brill wrinkled his nose. "I know that you and the princess became friends, but I certainly do not want to see Grossder. He never thought of anyone but himself." Brill stood. "Let us go to the bow so we can see where we are going."

They watched as the ship sailed toward the open sea. Waves crashed over the bow where Segra and Brill stood. Segra grabbed for the railing and hung on tightly so she could stand upright on the shifting deck.

"Here comes a splasher," she said. They laughed as the spray showered them with salty drops.

By afternoon the sun had disappeared behind gray clouds and the blue green water turned the color of lead. The wind blew hard, billowing the sails and making the old ship creak.

They sat in their sheltered spot until the captain shouted at them. "You two—get below. It is not safe on deck."

"Is a storm coming?" asked Segra.

He scowled at her. "The storm has already caught up with us. One of those big waves could pitch you right off the deck."

Segra shivered. She hurried to help Brill carry their belongings and food into the cargo section of the hold.

"This is as bad as a dungeon." Segra looked around the dark, smelly hold, crowded with sacks of grain.

"It will not be for long. By tomorrow the storm will be over, and we can go back to fresh air." Brill sounded hopeful.

Segra took shallow breaths to avoid smelling the odors of animal skins, stale cooking, and dirty clothes, but nothing helped. The ship pitched and tossed all night. She lay awake, fighting seasickness. Dizziness swept over her, and finally she staggered to a nearby bucket to empty the contents of her stomach.

In the flickering light of the oil lamp, she saw that Brill was asleep, apparently unaware of the sailors' worried shouts. Suddenly the lamp went out.

"Quep went overboard!" one man yelled.

"Are you sure?"

"Yes. Poor Quep! We were trying to secure the cargo. I have never seen the sea so rough."

"I hope this old ship will hold together."

"Even the sailors are afraid!" Segra murmured to herself. She curled herself into a tight ball and tried once more to sleep.

Finally, pale morning light filtered down into the dark hold. "I am going to get some fresh air," said Segra. She climbed the ladder to the deck. But she found that rain was pouring down, and the wind had whipped the waves into a frenzy of whitecapped breakers.

"Better not stay here," warned Iba. "We have already lost two men, and the storm is not over yet."

"I need air," Segra gasped. She breathed in the rain-washed air and felt better, but she had to grab the handle of a storage chest to keep from sliding across the slippery deck.

The captain shouted at her above the noise of the howling winds. "Get below before you get tossed overboard!"

Segra almost fell as she lurched across the wet, unsteady deck toward the ladder. Down in the hold, she found Brill munching a piece of dry bread.

"How can you eat?" she demanded crossly.

"I was hungry," he answered. "Would you like some bread?"

Segra shook her head. "No, I have been sick all night."

"I am sorry, Segra."

"I tried to go up on deck, but Iba made me come back. I am scared, Brill. I fear the wind and waves will sink this boat."

"The storm is getting worse." Brill scrambled out of the way as three large grain sacks fell off the pile. "We must get out of here before we get buried."

Brill took her hand as they dodged falling grain sacks and headed for the ladder. They climbed hurriedly, and Segra heard a sailor shout, "We almost flipped over that time."

As she and Brill crawled onto the deck, everyone was too busy to pay any attention to them. Segra looked around for Lopet, but she saw neither him nor his uncle. She grabbed the railing and hung on.

"If we are going down, I do not want to be trapped in that hold!" cried Brill.

Segra nodded, but she thought it would not be any better to drown in the open sea. The sky was a sheet of rain, and wave after wave slammed across the deck. She stared into the rain and glimpsed an island on the starboard side. Then she caught sight of the biggest wave she had ever seen.

"Brill, a big wave is coming!" she gasped.

The wave tossed the ship up on one end, and it hung quivering in the air. Segra held on as tightly as she could, but her cold hands slipped from the rail, and she plunged sideways, down into the ocean.

Frantically she thrashed her arms and legs, trying to get her head above water. Long ago, her father had taught her to swim, and now his words came back to her— "Relax, the water will hold you."

She rose to the surface and quickly gulped some air. The ship was lying on its side like a broken toy. She swam away from it.

Brill's face appeared for an instant. "Head for the island," he shouted. "I think it is this way." Then he disappeared in the waves.

She swam in the direction he had gone, sometimes catching sight of the island, but it looked impossibly far away. Waves splashed over her, tossing her about as if she were a tiny piece of driftwood. The weight of her woolen cloak pulled her down. Finally she unfastened the cloak and let it go, but she still had trouble with her legs tangling in her long dress.

She wondered what had happened to all the others. Perhaps they had gone down with the ship. Or perhaps the waves hid them. She feared she was not even swimming toward the island. It was difficult to tell directions.

A faint call sounded across the waves. "Help!"
She looked around but did not see anyone. She would
have liked to scream for help, too.

A wave lifted her, and she saw a thick plank
holding the boy, Lopet. He was calling out to her.

"I will lose too much time trying to reach him,"
she argued with herself. "I have to keep swimming
to the island. That is my only chance."

But she turned and swam toward the spot where
she had seen Lopet.

Brill's voice followed her. "Segra, you are going
the wrong way. Segra!" Then his voice was lost in
the howling wind.

She kept swimming toward the boy, trying to
keep him in sight as the waves tossed her about.
Finally she could reach out and grab the bobbing
plank. Lopet stared at her with terrified brown eyes.
He lay on his stomach, hugging the board with his
arms.

"Uncle Iba put me here," he gasped. "He was
trying to steer, but he fell off and went under the
water. I am so scared."

"Do not worry—you will be all right, Lopet,"
Segra said, wishing she could believe her own words.

The first thing she had to do was figure out a way to steer the plank. With both hands she grasped one end of it, then kicked vigorously, trying to steer it into the waves rather than meeting them sideways. But a large wave engulfed them, breaking Segra's hold. She fought to regain her spot at the end of the plank. "Hang on, Lopet," she shouted.

"I am cold," he cried.

"I know. We will build a fire as soon as we get to the island." But the island looked as far away as ever. Segra could not see Brill or anyone else from the ship. She wondered how long Lopet's little arms could hang on as he straddled the pitching plank.

"Lopet, try to kick so you will get warmer."

"I am too tired."

"It will help the plank go faster."

"I cannot." Lopet was sobbing, but Segra did not know how to reassure him when she felt like crying herself. Her legs were numb from the icy water, but she kept kicking. She imagined wading ashore on a sandy beach. Brill would light a fire and she would warm her frozen limbs. "Keep kicking, keep kicking!" she told herself over and over again. She still had a long way to go.

5
Shipwrecked

Off in the distance rose a gray shadow. It grew larger as they neared it. The island! Now Segra could see the gleam of a fire. She inhaled ragged breaths, seeking the strength to keep kicking.

"Look!" she exclaimed to Lopet, "There is the island—and a fire on the beach! I think Brill is already there."

The little boy did not answer. She pulled herself up onto the plank to look at him. "Are you all right?"

A wave broke over the plank, washing Lopet off. "Lopet!" Segra screamed. She dived after him, found nothing, and came up, gasping for breath. For a moment she hung on to the plank. Was it hopeless? No! She forced herself to dive again. As she surfaced, she blinked her stinging eyes. Was that a head? She swam toward the bobbing object, afraid it would disappear before she reached it.

"Lopet!" Breathless, she put an arm around his chest so that his face was out of the water, but he hung limp in the waves. She kicked her legs and stroked with her free arm.

The island was not coming any closer. Her one-armed swimming was too weak to overcome the waves and current.

Then she heard Brill's voice. "I will take him."

"Oh—thank you!" She let the boy slide into Brill's arms and floated for a minute to regain her strength.

Brill clutched Lopet and headed for shore. "There is a heavy surf," he warned over his shoulder. "But you can do it."

Wearily, Segra began swimming again. She kicked her hardest through the tall breakers and fought the undertow that tried to pull her back out to sea. Suddenly she was in knee-deep water, with sand under her feet. She crawled onto the beach, lying exhausted for a few minutes on the cold, wet sand. Then she forced herself to walk to the driftwood fire Brill had made with his fire stones.

Brill was rubbing Lopet's chilled limbs. "Is he breathing?" she gasped.

"Yes, but he is still unconscious. I think he will be all right when he warms up."

"I hope so." Segra knelt beside the little boy and stretched out her numbed hands to the fire. The rain had stopped, but the wind still howled, whipping through the evergreen trees. Brill had collected a pile of driftwood and built the fire next to a large rock, so they had some shelter from the wind.

"Have you seen anyone else?" she asked.

"No. We seem to be the only ones here."

"Do you think all the others drowned?"

"Some may have reached other islands, or perhaps they are still out there floating on pieces of wreckage."

Brill had spread his cloak over a piece of driftwood. Segra felt sorry she had dropped hers in the sea, but with the extra weight, she might not have made it to shore.

As Brill added more wood to the fire, he asked, "Where did you pick up Lopet?"

"Near the ship."

"How did you swim so far with him?"

"He was on a plank. I pushed it." Segra shook out her hair over the fire, separating the wet strands with her fingers.

"I kept yelling at you until I was hoarse. Then you disappeared. I was afraid you had drowned. I should have guessed you were trying to help someone."

"I could not leave Lopet. I wish he would wake up."

Brill put his hand on the boy's forehead. "He feels a little warmer than when I first brought him out of the water."

Segra shifted her position so her cold side could have a turn at the fire's warmth. Her soaked dress was drying—stiff from its saltwater bath. Beneath it, she felt the bulge made by the sack of jewels, still fastened to her waist. She was thankful it had not come loose in the water.

Lopet squirmed. Segra watched to be sure he did not get too close to the fire. Then he cried out, "The water is swallowing me. Help! Uncle Iba, help!"

Segra put her arm around the trembling boy. "Lopet, you are only dreaming. You are safe now."

He opened his eyes. "My board. Where is my board?"

"You are on the beach. You do not need a board."

He felt the sand with his hand. "The water swallowed Uncle Iba." Tears rolled down his cheeks. "Where is Mama?"

"She is in Magra. You were on a trip. Remember?"

He nodded. "I am thirsty. May I have a drink?"

"We do not have any water," answered Brill.

Lopet pointed to the ocean. "There is lots of water."

"That is salt water," Segra explained. "You cannot drink it. It would make you sick."

"The tide is out," said Brill. "I will try to dig some clams. I am starving."

Segra sighed. "I do not want to leave this fire."

"You stay with Lopet. I will see what I can find."

Lopet took his shoes off, put his bare feet close to the fire, and wiggled his toes.

"Good idea." Segra took off her waterlogged shoes and pointed her feet at the fire. "My feet feel like blocks of ice."

"Mine are prickly."

"That means they are getting warm."

"How will we get to Magra?" asked Lopet.

"We will figure out a way."

When Brill returned, he carried a dozen medium-sized clams. "I will put them close to the fire until they pop open." He arranged the clams by the coals, and as soon as they were hot, he offered the first ones to Segra and Lopet.

Lopet shook his head as he looked at the sandy clams.

Segra pulled the meat from the shell, trying to brush off the sand.

Brill chewed on a clam with obvious enjoyment. "Take all you want. I can dig more."

"Thanks." Segra ate three, but she was more thirsty than hungry. "After we have rested, let us explore the island."

"I hope we find a village with a well and a marketplace," said Brill. "Maybe we can get passage on a ship to take us to Magra."

"This might be Pover, Brill. Iba said we would be sailing by it."

Brill scowled. "I do not want to see Grossder again."

"He cannot order you around as he did when he was an emprince. I would like to see Florette. We were good friends."

In the afternoon they began to explore the island, hoping they might find water and something edible. Segra's throat was dry from thirst.

"Maybe we will find a chest of gold." Lopet's eyes shone at the prospect.

"I would rather find a chest of bread and honey," said Brill. "You cannot eat gold."

Lopet ran ahead to explore some tide pools at a rocky point. "I see a crab," he called.

Brill ran over to look. "That is not even bite size."

As the sun burned off the mist, Segra looked up at the rest of the island. It was hilly and covered with trees, except for the beach. She called, "Brill, come here."

"Did you find something to eat?"

"No, but I see a column of smoke. Someone else is on this island." She pointed to a hilltop.

"Come on, maybe they will invite us for dinner." Brill led as they walked along the beach looking for a path to lead them up the hillside. The beach narrowed, and they looked up at a steep stone cliff.

Segra stopped. "I do not think there will be a beach here at high tide. Look, you can see the tide line on the cliff. Maybe we should go back."

"If we hurry, we can get beyond this narrow beach before the tide covers it," said Brill confidently. He hoisted Lopet up onto his shoulder. They walked faster.

The cliff became lower until the forest was level with the beach. They rounded a small cape and discovered a cove sheltered from the surf by a breakwater of rocks.

"Look," cried Brill. "A rowboat."

Segra glanced at it. "It will not float. Too many missing boards." She turned toward the woods. "But here is a path." Brill and Lopet followed her, and the path sloped gently upward.

"I want to get down," said Lopet, so Brill lifted him down from his shoulder.

They had been hiking only a few minutes when they heard a cross voice. "Halt! Lay down your arms."

"We are not armed. We have been shipwrecked," called Brill. He turned to Segra. "I know that voice. It is Grossder."

"I thought we might be on Pover," Segra whispered.

"Proceed up the path slowly," the voice ordered.

They walked cautiously up the path. Lopet reached for Segra's hand and gripped it tightly.

Grossder stepped out from behind a large tree trunk. "So, it is Brill. I guess you did not expect to see me again." He had lost some of the weight he gained during his years as emprince of Exitorn.

Then Grossder drew his bow and aimed an arrow at them.

"Do not shoot us. We are friends." Brill's voice sounded shaky.

Grossder scowled. "You and Segra are traitors. If it had not been for you, I would still be an emprince."

"The people were rising against your father's rule," Segra reminded him. "Even if Brill and I had not helped, the revolution would have taken place."

"The people wanted a ruler who understood their problems and would try to help them," Brill added.

"Do not talk about Father." Grossder dropped the arrow from his bow and began to cry in great choking sobs.

"What is the matter?" Segra asked.

Grossder sniffled. "Father drowned when he went out in the rowboat to fish. It is all your fault."

"We are sorry about your father—" Segra began.

"Grossder, who are you talking to?"

"Florette!" Segra dropped Lopet's hand and ran up the path.

Florette threw her arms around her. "Segra! What are you doing on Pover?"

"We were shipwrecked. This is our friend, Lopet."

"Come up to the house and see Mother," said Florette. "She will invite you for dinner."

Grossder stamped his foot. "Florette!" he cried. "We cannot feed these traitors! It is because of them that we are stuck here."

Florette frowned at her brother. "I should think you would be glad to see someone else. It is lonely here."

She led them to a clearing where a small wooden house stood, and Lopet ran straight to the well.

"We are very thirsty," Brill explained.

"Help yourself," said Florette. Brill lowered a bucket, drew up fresh water, and gave Lopet the first drink. Segra drank next. Never had water tasted so good.

When they were satisfied, they followed Florette into the two-room cottage.

Lera, the former queen, greeted them warmly. "Of course you are welcome here. We will have dinner soon—there is plenty of fish and rice." She motioned for them to sit down at the wooden table.

When it was ready, she dished up the meal from a kettle hanging on a hook over the fire. Segra smiled as the warm food settled comfortably in her hollow stomach.

Between bites, she and Brill told the story of their shipwreck. Lopet sat without saying a word, eating steadily. Brill ended the tale. "The next time a ship comes here, we hope to sail to Magra to find Segra's and Lopet's parents."

Grossder snickered. "A ship with supplies will come by in a year or so, maybe. You are stuck here just like us."

"Ships do not stop here?" asked Brill.

"No. Pover was a deserted island before we came."

Brill groaned. "We cannot stay here for a whole year."

Segra frowned at Grossder, who grinned at them as if he were enjoying their despair. "We must find a way to get to Magra so I can look for my parents."

"I saw a rowboat on the beach," said Brill. "Perhaps I can fix it with driftwood boards. Do you have any nails?"

"We have nails and a hammer, but you will never get that wreck to float," predicted Grossder.

"That is the boat that failed poor Father," Florette cried. "It broke up on the rocks. You cannot go out in that!"

"Nor can we sit here waiting for the supply ship." Brill reached for another slice of bread.

"You will not be sitting," pointed out Grossder. "You will be looking for food. It is not easy to find enough to eat on Pover."

The former queen began clearing the table. "You must stay with us and share our food."

"Mother!" cried Grossder. "We cannot feed three more people. We will run out of food before the supply ship comes."

"Grossder, do not be so selfish," scolded Florette.

"We will not stay here any longer than we have to," Brill said. "I am going to fix that boat."

Lopet spoke up suddenly. "And I will help you!"

"When we get back to Exitorn, we will tell the king that Emperor Immane is dead," promised Segra. "I am sure King Talder will let you return from exile."

Grossder's eyes brightened. "I hope the rowboat does not dump you into the sea. I would like to get off this miserable island."

Segra did not like the thought of bouncing over those waves in a tiny rowboat. "Brill," she said quietly, "I hope you and Lopet do a very good job on that boat."

6
The Meladora Tale

The next day after Segra and Florette had washed the breakfast dishes, they walked down to the beach. "Do you remember this dress?" Segra asked.

Florette shook her head as she looked at the tattered blue garment.

"It is the dress I put on when we changed places in prison. I cut off the jewels and sold some of them, but you may have the rest. They belong to you." Segra reached for the bag of jewels.

"No, Segra, keep the jewels!" cried Florette. "You will need them on your journey. Mother and I have other jeweled dresses packed away. If we get back to Exitorn, we still will have enough for living expenses."

"Are you certain?"

"Yes, I am." Florette pulled her cloak tightly around her as the wind blew from the sea. "Where is your cloak?" she asked.

"It was too heavy to swim in after the shipwreck, so I unfastened it and let it sink."

"I will give you a cloak," said Florette. "We brought all our clothes with us, so we have plenty."

"Thank you. I do miss my cloak."

When they stepped onto the sand, they saw Grossder crouching behind a driftwood log. He put an arrow in his bow as a huge white bird with silver-tipped wings flew toward the beach.

Segra stared at the bird in astonishment. It was at least twice as big as an eagle, with wings that spread more than twelve feet.

The bird circled downward, skimmed the sand, then glided onto the beach.

Grossder pulled his bow string back.

"No, Grossder. Do not shoot!" Segra cried. At the sound of her voice, the bird lifted off, its huge, powerful wings taking it out of range in a few seconds.

"What are you doing?" said Grossder. "You spoiled a good shot."

"It is a beautiful bird. How can you want to kill it?"

"It would have made a delicious meal. Foolish girl! We cannot survive unless we find food on the island. With three extra people, we will run out of supplies long before the ship comes back."

"We can survive without that bird," insisted Segra. "Please, Grossder, promise me you will not kill it."

"I will not make any such promise. The only fun I have in this miserable place is shooting my arrows. It feels good to kill an animal or a bird and know that I am helping to supply our food."

"You are a good shot," Florette said. "But it would be a shame to eat such an unusual bird."

"I will kill it, and you will all enjoy eating it." Grossder searched the sky, looking for the bird.

Segra watched him, wishing she could think of some way to make the bird understand that it was not safe here.

Lopet and Brill came running down the path. "I saw a meladora bird!" cried Lopet.

"What kind?" asked Segra.

"A meladora. No one has seen one for almost a hundred years."

"Then how do you know what it was?" asked Florette.

"It is just like my grandmother described—huge and white, with silver on its wings. Grandmother never saw one, but her father told her what they looked like."

Brill said, "Lopet started to tell me his grandmother's story, but I said he should wait until the rest of you could hear it also."

"Tell us, Lopet," said Segra. She and Florette sat on a driftwood log. Florette unfastened her cloak and put it around Segra too. Brill lifted Lopet up onto a large rock and then joined the girls on the log.

Grossder muttered, "I do not have time to listen to a story about a bird. I need to hunt if we are to eat." He shuffled off.

Lopet sat for a minute, as if to remember just how the story began. Finally he said, "The meladora birds lived on an island way out in the ocean." He pointed to the open sea. "They nested in the tall trees on a mountain that was really a volcano. It was in the middle of the island. A tribe of people lived on the lower part of the island. The men were fishermen, and the women tended vegetable gardens.

"One day a little boy named Banette wandered off into the thick forest. He was about two years old. No one could find him. All the people spread through the forest calling, 'Banette? Banette?' They called again and again. But no one answered. After they had searched for seven days, they gave up. Only his mother and father kept looking. Finally they had to go home too, but they were scratched and bleeding, and heartsick because their only child was lost.

"The father went back to sea, and the mother sat in front of her house weeping for Banette. Suddenly a large meladora bird flew down in front of her, holding Banette in its long, curved talons. Gently the bird set the boy on the ground, and his mother ran to him. She picked him up and hugged him.

"The little boy looked up at her and said, 'Mama! A big bird helped me.'

"She cried with joy and called, 'Thank you! Oh, thank you!' to the bird, but it was already flying away."

"That is a lovely story," said Segra.

"I am not finished," said Lopet. "The people on the island were so thankful to the meladora bird that they began putting out food for the birds on the flat roofs of their houses. The birds flew down in the early evening to pick up tidbits of shellfish or grains and vegetables from the gardens.

"After that, the meladoras watched out for the fishermen. If one of them saw a boat in trouble, it would fly to the nearest boat and sit on the mast with its beak pointing to the boat in danger. The fisherman knew he should sail toward the troubled boat."

"How do you know all this?" asked Brill.

"I am getting to that," answered Lopet. "When Banette grew up, he built his own fishing boat and went to sea. One terrible day he watched the volcano erupt, burying the whole island in hot ash. Banette tried to sail into the choking ash cloud to look for his wife and small son, but the closer he came to the island, the thicker the ash grew, and he was afraid his boat would run into the rocks. Then a meladora bird swooped down and placed his four-year-old son on the deck of Banette's boat.

"Banette hugged his son and cried, 'Where is your mother?'

" 'In the water,' answered the boy.

"The bird seemed to understand what they said. It dipped its wings as if to say 'Follow me.' Banette steered his boat into the cloud of ash, and the bird kept doubling back to lead him in the right direction.

"When Banette saw the frightened people swimming, he began to help them aboard. He found out that the birds had picked up all the younger children. The mothers, older children, and other people who were too heavy for the birds had started swimming away from the island, hoping to find the boats. The birds had guided the boats to the swimmers, and soon everyone was picked up. Banette found his wife, and his family had a joyful reunion.

"Later his wife said, 'Banette, you must write down the story of the meladoras and how they helped us.' And that is what he did. For years and years, it has been copied and recopied."

"What happened to the birds?" asked Florette.

"Their high island home was gone, so they flew away, but no one knows where. Meladoras can fly long distances."

"And to think that we saw one today!" Florette stood. "I will talk to Grossder and tell him why he must not shoot the big bird. But he will probably not listen to me."

"Did the people ever go back to their island?" asked Segra.

"No, they had to live on the coast of Magra or on the nearby islands. They kept on fishing. My grandmother said Banette was my great-great-grandfather. I always hoped that one day I would see a meladora bird."

In the days that followed, life on the little island settled into a routine. Brill worked on the rowboat. He and Lopet tramped the beaches looking for wood from shipwrecks to replace its missing boards.

Grossder did not walk far from the house. His only contribution was an occasional rabbit or seabird. Sometimes Segra saw the meladora bird flying above her or resting in one of the trees. She hoped the bird would stay out of Grossder's sight.

Segra and Florette hiked through the woods looking for edible roots. They dug clams and pried mussels from the rocks on the beach. One day Segra found a strange shell in a tide pool, and she called Florette.

"Look, it is two balls fastened together," said Segra.

"That is a double-bubble shell. It is hard to find them, but they are very good eating—lots of sweet meat."

"Florette, how do you know so much about shells?"

"Mother taught me. She grew up near the sea. Without her, we would not know what was good food and what was poisonous."

Segra pried the double-bubble shell from the rock to which it was fastened and put it in her basket of shells.

One day when they did not need to gather food, Segra and Florette watched Brill cutting boards and fitting them to the bottom of the boat. Lopet stayed close to him, eager to help. "You are making good progress," said Segra.

The days passed slowly for Segra, even though she kept busy gathering food and wood. She often thought of her parents. Perhaps they had returned to Exitorn by now. Her desire to get off the island grew stronger than her fear of the waves.

Two weeks later at breakfast, Brill announced that he was ready to launch the repaired boat.

Segra frowned. "Do you think water will leak between the boards?"

"Lopet and I put plenty of pitch on it. As far as I can tell, it is waterproof."

"But what about the waves that will splash up into it?" Florette asked.

"Today is fairly calm. I have been watching the water. Some days are much calmer than others."

"Are you going to fish?" asked Grossder.

"Not the first day. But if the boat works all right, I will go fishing."

"Good," said Florette. "I would rather eat fish than fishy-tasting birds."

"You should be glad I shoot birds. But I wish I could get that big one." Grossder scowled at Segra. "It has never come close since that day you scared it."

"A wise bird it is," she said.

Segra, Florette, and Lopet walked down to the sheltered cove with Brill. He pushed his boat out, gripped the oars, and headed for the opening in the breakwater where he would meet the ocean waves.

Segra thought of how the wind had blown until their big ship capsized. This boat looked too frail to face the large waves.

They watched from the beach until Brill returned with a triumphant smile. "It works fine." He pulled the boat up onto the sand.

"May I go for a ride?" asked Lopet.

"Not until I have had more experience with the waves." Brill picked up Lopet and balanced him on his shoulders. "See that island across the channel? That is where we are going one of these days."

"I want to go to Magra."

"We will get there—one island at a time."

Segra sighed. "Is it wise to leave Pover when we do not know what is on that other island?"

"Segra, you were always the adventurous one. What has happened?"

"I still have nightmares about drowning."

"Stay with me, Segra," begged Florette. "When a big ship comes, we will all go home."

Segra looked at the small, patched boat. She did not trust it, but she could not let Brill go alone. He might need her help. "I must go, Florette."

For the next few days, the ocean was relatively calm. Brill went out in the boat each day, often returning with a catch of fish.

One afternoon as Segra strolled down the path, she heard Brill and Grossder arguing.

"I risk my life every day fishing," Brill said. "The least you could do is help me clean the fish."

"I am an emprince."

"Not any more."

"I will always be an emprince. I was born an emprince."

"When you were born, your father was an ordinary fellow. He fought King Talder and took his throne until the people revolted. You are back to being an ordinary fellow, and you ought to do your share of work. Even Lopet gathers wood and digs clams."

"I hate slimy clams. I wish you would take that boat and leave," said Grossder.

"We will go on the next calm day."

Grossder tramped up the path, not bothering to answer Segra's greeting. She joined Brill. "There is no use arguing with Grossder."

"He annoys me. I like to say what I think after being so careful not to make him angry when I lived in the palace."

"You will not change him by arguing. The Book of Wisdom says, *Be kind to everyone. That is the best way to be happy.*"

"I will be glad to leave here. The boat handles well."

Segra sighed. "I want to see Mother and Father so much."

"After we find your parents, we will all go back to Exitorn, and I will go home again."

"Oh, Brill, I know you miss your parents. I am sorry I took you so far from home for such a long time."

"It is not your fault that it is taking so long." He looked at the sky. "I will be up every morning, checking the weather. On the first fair day we will leave."

"It will be marvelous to get off this island!" Segra exclaimed. To herself she said, "I will not let myself think about the waves."

When Florette came to the beach, Segra told her their plans.

"Oh, Segra, I will miss you terribly."

"When we get back to Exitorn, we will send a ship to rescue you."

The next few days were stormy, with strong wind and heavy rain. On the second day of the storm, Lera fainted as she was fixing breakfast. After she revived, Florette and Segra helped her back to bed.

"Mother, what is the matter?" asked Florette.

"I feel a little ill this morning. I will be better after I rest."

Segra put a hand on her forehead. "You seem too warm."

"I may have a slight fever—nothing serious."

The girls finished the breakfast preparations, but Lera wanted only water.

As Segra drew more water, Florette said, "I know your father taught you how to help sick people. Can you cure Mother?"

"There is an herb called glondine that can bring down a fever," Segra said, "but I do not know if it grows here. I will see if I can find any. That is the only thing I know that might help."

Segra put on the cloak Florette had given her and tramped through the wet woods looking for the healing herb. She walked as far as the beach on the south side of the island, but she saw no glondine. Finally she returned, soaking wet and discouraged.

Lera grew worse. That night her face was burning hot, and she raved in delirium. Segra and Florette began to fear for her life.

Early the next morning, Segra started out again to search for glondine. This time she trudged through the woods toward the cliffs. She studied the first cliff. Growing among the weeds at the top were tiny purple flowers that looked like glondine.

Carefully she began to climb the steep face of the rock, wedging her toes into holes and grasping at rocky handholds. She was halfway up when the wall of rock became so rough that she could climb no higher.

In her frustration she cried aloud. "Surely that is glondine! There it is—just out of my reach. What am I going to do?"

Heavy wings beat over her head, and she looked up. The meladora bird swooped down and plucked a sprig of glondine with his beak. He dropped it at the foot of the cliff.

"Oh, thank you," Segra called. "Now Florette's mother will get well. Thank you!"

He dipped his head and circled twice above the cliff before flying off.

Segra watched him go. "I am going to call you Stargull because your wings look strong enough to fly to the stars," she said. He was much too big for a gull, and his talons looked like the claws of an eagle, but still she liked the name. *Stargull.*

Hurriedly she climbed down the cliff and picked up the glondine plant, then returned to the house to brew its leaves into tea.

Lera was still delirious, but Segra and Florette propped her up, and she drank the warm tea.

After her mother went back to sleep, Florette asked, "How long will it take the herb to make Mother feel better?"

"I am not sure. We will give her the tea every few hours."

When Grossder came in for lunch, Segra told him how the meladora bird had picked the herb that was helping his mother.

Grossder shook his head. "I do not believe that bird knew what you wanted."

Florette cried, "If you had shot the bird, Mother might have died."

Lera continued to moan and thrash about during the second night, but once in a while, she slept. Segra and Florette took turns soothing her and giving her sips of tea.

They gave her more tea the next morning and watched as she slipped again into a restless sleep.

Brill rushed in and whispered to Segra, "The weather is perfect. Let us go today."

Segra shook her head. "I cannot leave until Lera is better."

"Florette can take care of her. I have never seen the sea as calm as it is today."

"You go, Brill."

"I am not going to leave you. I wish you would think of yourself first once in a while."

"You do not mean that."

"Yes, I do. You are always helping somebody— King Talder, Peachy, the boy beaten by robbers, Lopet—I cannot even remember them all. But I guess that is why everyone likes you so much."

"There will be another good day."

"I hope so," Brill said slowly.

7
Dangerous Crossing

A few nights later, Lera's fever broke. Segra bent over the sleeping woman and pulled a blanket to her chin. "We do not want her to get a chill," she whispered to Florette.

The next day Lera sat up long enough to sip a bit of soup. "I am so weak," she murmured.

"You have been sick for almost a week," Segra told her. "Perhaps you should stay in bed for a while longer."

Grossder came in with a gull he had shot. "Mother, can you make this into that stew I like?"

Florette glared at him. "Mother cannot cook yet."

Lera struggled to sit up. "Maybe if I sat on a chair—"

"No, Mother. You must rest until you feel fine," said Florette. "Grossder will have to survive on our cooking."

That afternoon as Segra walked on the beach, Brill joined her. "Can we go, now that Lera is better?"

"Florette needs some help until her mother is stronger."

Brill stopped at the boat. "I think we should go the first day the sea is reasonably calm."

Segra hesitated. "I suppose Florette could manage the cooking for a while. All right, Brill, we will go when you say the word."

Three days later, in the early light of dawn, Brill climbed the ladder to the loft where Segra and Florette slept. "Segra," he whispered.

She awoke instantly. "Is Florette's mother worse?"

"No. The weather is perfect. Let us leave."

Segra scrambled up. "Today it is."

After a hasty breakfast, Brill, Segra, and Lopet gathered their few belongings and said good-bye.

Lera held out a thin hand to Segra. "Thank you for taking care of me."

"It was my pleasure."

"Florette, put some bread and smoked clams in a bag for their journey," said her mother.

"I already did." Florette handed Segra a cloth bag. "I put in an extra dress so you will have something better to wear when you find your father and mother."

"Thank you." Segra's eyes filled with tears as she hugged Florette.

Down at the cove, Brill pushed the boat partway into the water and Segra and Lopet climbed into it.

"Tell someone to come and get us in a big ship," Grossder called.

"We will," promised Brill. He gave the boat a hard shove and jumped in as it slid free of the sand.

Segra tried not to worry Brill took control of the oars. She moved to the bow seat so she could watch for rocks.

"This is fun," Lopet said from his seat in the stern.

When they left the sheltered cove, the water became rougher. Segra did not like the way the waves picked up the boat, then dropped it into the troughs between swells. Soon she was soaking wet from the splashing waves.

Brill steered across the waves toward the green island in the distance.

"Brill, that island looks a long way off," said Segra.

"We will make it."

"Look!" Lopet yelled. "Sharks."

Segra gazed at the dark triangles cutting the water. "Why are they following us?"

"Do not worry," said Brill. "They cannot get at us—not in the boat."

Segra kept her eyes on the shark fins, hoping a big wave would not overturn their small boat.

"Lopet, I am appointing you mate in charge of bailing," said Brill. "Too much water has splashed into the boat."

Lopet grabbed a small pan and began dumping the water from the bottom of the boat back into the sea. "This is too hard," he complained after a while. "No matter how much water I dump out, there is always more."

"You are doing a fine job," Brill assured him. "Take a little rest, then try it again."

The sharks stopped following them, and Segra began to breathe a little easier. She kept watching the island. "Brill," she asked suddenly, "why are we getting farther away?"

"We are caught in a strong current. I am rowing as hard as I can, but we are being pulled out to sea."

Segra gripped the side of the boat and stared at the lapping waves. She remembered how close she and Lopet had come to drowning after the shipwreck. "Brill, let me help you row," she cried.

"You can try."

She crept to the middle of the boat and sat down beside Brill. Then she grasped one oar with both hands and pulled as hard as she could.

"We have to get a rhythm going." Brill began to count. "1, 2, 3—stroke."

Segra concentrated on her rowing, trying to match Brill's strokes and keep her oar from skimming the surface or from going into the water too deeply.

"We are getting closer," she said at last.

"I think we have finally crossed the current." Brill turned to Lopet. "Your job is to watch for rocks, mate." He reached for Lopet's hand and helped him move to the bow.

"No rocks, Captain," Lopet called.

"Keep looking."

Lopet yelled, "I see smoke on the island. Somebody is there!"

"You are right," Segra exclaimed. "I cannot see any houses. They must be on the other side." She straightened her skirt. The bright sun had partially dried her clothes, even though it was a cool day.

"Can we eat lunch when we land?" asked Lopet.

"First thing," agreed Brill. "I am starved."

"Looks like mostly large rocks on shore," observed Brill. "We need a sandy place to land. I do not want the boat to smash on the rocks."

As they came closer, Lopet kept calling, "Go right," or "Go left," to help them avoid rocks.

Since the rowing was easier now, Segra moved to the stern to bail. The cool water felt good to her sore hands. She glanced up. Where had that big bird come from? It was Stargull! He was gliding down toward them. "Brill, look—the meladora bird! Perhaps he is leading us to a good landing place."

Brill eyed the huge bird. "You think he is as intelligent as your dinogator friends?"

"Yes, I do. Remember Lopet's story about the meladoras helping people? Follow him, Brill."

"I guess that way is as good as any." He rowed along the shoreline until they came to steep cliffs rising from the water. "No place to land here," observed Brill. "Are you sure that bird knows what we want?"

"Stargull, we need a place to land our boat," called Segra.

He dipped his wings and flew lower, doubling back every so often, until they reached a sheltered harbor. A fishing boat was moored by a large wooden dock. Built against the steep hillside were a dozen houses.

"We made it," cried Brill.

"Thank you, Stargull," called Segra. She waved at the bird, who rose higher and higher, the sunlight glinting on his silvery wings.

Brill guided the boat to the dock and tied it to a post.

"Well, Brill," said Segra, "you have accomplished a remarkable feat—repairing the boat and crossing to this island."

He grinned. "I am glad we made it safely."

"When can we eat?" asked Lopet.

"We will find a place," promised Brill. Together they started down the dock.

An old man limped out to the end of the dock and looked at them suspiciously. "Where are you from?"

"We just rowed over here from Pover."

The old man scowled. "Nobody lives on Pover except the exiled emperor of Exitorn and his family."

"We were shipwrecked," explained Brill.

"Can we get to Magra from here?" asked Segra.

"Water is too rough for a little boat like yours." The old man thought about it for a while. Finally he said, "One of the fishermen might take you. There is Gallet. He has the biggest boat, but he does not like strangers."

"Is he around?" asked Brill eagerly.

"No. He is out fishing." The man gave their little boat a puzzled frown. "How did you children ever get here? A strong current runs between us and Pover. The fishing boats avoid it."

"We rowed very hard." Brill held out his blistered hands. "When will Gallet be back?"

"Not until late afternoon—when the boats come in."

"Perhaps he can help us," Brill said. "Thank you, sir."

Brill, Segra, and Lopet walked down to the rocky beach. They sat on a driftwood log and ate smoked clams and black bread. When they were finished, Segra slipped away and hiked up the beach to a grove of trees. There she pulled out her sack of jewels and selected a pearl. Perhaps Gallet would accept it as payment to take them to Magra.

When the fishing boats began to return, Brill, Segra, and Lopet hurried to the dock and asked questions until they found Gallet. "Will you take us to Magra in your boat?" asked Brill.

Gallet, a tall, muscular man, looked down at them and frowned. "Six tencoins is my price," he said, as if he were sure they could never pay it.

"I can give you a pearl worth much more than that," offered Segra.

"And where would you get a pearl?" he demanded.

"I once worked for the princess of Exitorn. She gave it to me."

"Let me see."

Segra opened her hand to reveal the large, perfect pearl.

His gray eyes brightened. "With that I could impress the headman's daughter. I will take you to Molter—Magra's capital—first thing in the morning."

That night Brill, Segra, and Lopet slept on the deck of Gallet's boat. The next day was cloudy with a brisk wind.

Gallet put up his sail, and they sailed out of the harbor toward the mainland. The smell of fish was strong in the wooden boat. Yesterday's catch lay in a deep container of sea water that would keep it cool and fresh.

"I am going to sell my fish at Molter," Gallet explained.

"How long will it take to get there?" asked Segra.

"If this wind keeps up, we will be there by afternoon. And I hope it does. My fish do not improve with age." Gallet laughed loudly.

In the late afternoon they arrived at Molter, a bustling town built on a peninsula. A stone castle stood at the end of the peninsula, walled off from the rest of the city.

Gallet tied his boat to one of the busy docks where fishermen and traders shouted orders to their crews. Big burly men rushed about carrying cargo. Gallet put a gangplank between the boat and dock, and Brill, Segra, and Lopet hurried off.

Brill looked at Lopet. "Do you know where your house is?"

"Of course." Lopet pointed to a winding street leading from the harbor. "Follow me."

Brill and Segra had to run to keep up with the excited child. Finally Lopet stopped in front of a small wooden house and banged on the door. It opened a crack, then a short, thin woman rushed out and flung her arms around him. "Lopet, Lopet, I have been so worried." Tears of joy streamed down her face.

"There was a terrible storm, and the ship got turned over in the waves," he said. "And Uncle Iba put me on a plank in the water—"

"Where is your uncle?" she said.

"I do not know—I did not see him again, Mama."

"Oh, I fear for him. I am so sorry." Her eyes filled again with tears.

Lopet put a hand on her arm. "If it had not been for Segra and Brill, I would have drowned too."

She smiled at them. "I can never thank you enough. Lopet does not swim well, and he is so young—" She turned back to Lopet. "But your father—have you seen him?"

"No, Mama."

Lopet's mother looked anxiously toward the harbor. "Everyone said you must have drowned, but your father would not believe that. He keeps sailing among the islands to ask if anyone has seen you."

"I hope he comes back soon," said Lopet.

"Come inside," said his mother. "Come, Segra and Brill. What can I do for you? Would you like something to drink?"

"How long has Lopet's father been gone?" asked Segra.

Lopet's mother lowered her voice. "Over two weeks. I am very worried. It is dangerous to sail close to those rock islands." Then she spoke more loudly. "I will cook some beans. You must be hungry."

"Yes," Brill said. He was always hungry.

Lopet added, "They do not have a place to stay in Magra until they find Segra's papa and mama."

"You are welcome to stay here as long as you want," said Lopet's mother.

"We are from Exitorn," explained Segra. "We have come to look for my parents. They moved here because they thought I had been executed by the emperor."

"The trouble is," Brill said, "we do not know where to look."

"Quite a few people came from Exitorn to live in Magra," Lopet's mother said. "Most of them became sheep herders in the mountains."

"That must be where my parents are." Segra looked at her hopefully. "How far away are the mountains?"

"About forty miles across the farmland."

Brill groaned. "Another long hike."

"At least we will not have to worry about being shipwrecked," said Segra.

He shook his head, smiling. "No, all we have to think about are tired feet and robbers."

Segra could not find words to answer him, but she would not let herself feel discouraged. If Mother and Father were really there, forty miles did not seem so far.

8

Questions

That night Segra and Brill slept by the fire with Lopet and his mother. The earth floor was hard packed, and they wrapped themselves in wool blankets. It was an improvement, Segra thought, over the damp deck where they had slept the night before.

They were awakened before dawn by a loud knocking on the door.

Lopet's mother snatched up a candle and lit it from the coals in the fireplace.

Segra stared at the door, afraid that the knocking fist would break right through it. Who would be making such a noise at this time of night?

"Mama, I am afraid." Lopet jumped up and clutched his mother's skirt.

His mother stepped close to the door. The candle she held shook, and her voice trembled as she called, "Who—who is out there?"

A deep voice answered, "It is Vorn."

Quickly, she unbolted the door and pulled it open. A tall man stepped inside. The sadness on his face changed to joy as Lopet threw his arms around him. "Papa, Papa!"

"Lopet!" He lifted the boy in his arms. "I have looked all over for you. My dear son!" He hugged his wife. "Ah, Hallie, all those long hours I sailed my boat among the islands, I dreamed of the day we could all be together again."

No one slept anymore. Lopet's mother made tea, and as they sipped it, Lopet, Brill, and Segra retold the story of their shipwreck.

When they finished, Vorn said, "Poor Iba. We shall all miss him." He looked down at Lopet cuddled in his lap and said to Brill and Segra. "You have given me back my son, who is more precious to me than life itself. If there is anything I can ever do to help you, please ask."

"We are here on a search that is important to us," said Brill. "Do you know the way to the mountains where the Exitornians have settled?"

"I can draw you a map showing the roads to take. You are welcome to stay here as long as you like. We could take you around to see some of the sights of the capital."

Segra said, "We cannot stay. I am looking for my parents. They may be with the sheep herders from Exitorn."

Vorn nodded, as if he understood. "I hope you are as fortunate as I have been; may you be soon reunited with your family."

Early in the morning, Hallie packed food for them, and Brill and Segra continued their journey.

As they left the city, a chilly wind reminded them that winter was fast approaching. They traveled all day. That night they slept in a field of haystacks. They each chose a stack and burrowed into it to keep warm. Segra pulled her cloak tightly around her, trying to shield herself from the prickly stems of straw that jabbed at her whenever she moved. The dust made her sneeze, but finally she fell asleep.

The next morning they awoke with the sun and trudged on. By late afternoon they had arrived at a small town at the base of the mountains. Brill spoke to a farmer in the marketplace. "Can you tell me if there are any people from Exitorn living here?"

The man shook his head and went back to arranging squash and purple roots on a bench.

A woman working in an herb stall next to him spoke up. "They live up the valley. Keep to themselves mostly. Are you Exitornians?"

Brill nodded.

"The king will not let any more come here," said the farmer. "You had better go back where you came from."

"We are not staying," explained Segra. "When we find my parents, we will all go back to Exitorn."

The man gestured to his right. "The valley is up that road."

Brill and Segra set out, and the road soon narrowed to a winding path. For a mile or so, the path became steeper, then it leveled off and followed a small river. High mountains arose on either side. The growing darkness made it difficult to see where they were going.

"This must be the valley we are looking for," Segra said.

"I do not see any houses."

A gruff voice pierced the gloom. "Halt! Who goes there?"

They stopped. Segra stared at a dark figure on the rocks above them.

Brill spoke up. "We do not mean any harm. We are only—"

"Go back to town," the lookout ordered. "We do not want strangers in our valley."

"Do you know a couple named Garsil and Nalane?" Segra asked. "They are my parents."

"We have come a long way to find them," added Brill.

The man lit a lantern and jumped down from the rocks. "Are you from Exitorn?" he asked.

"Yes, we are. Please, tell me if Garsil and Nalane live here," cried Segra.

He held up the lantern and studied her face for a minute. "They did live here," he said at last. "But they are not here now. Come with me—people will want to hear the latest news from Exitorn."

Segra blinked back tears at this new disappointment. "Where have they gone?" she asked.

His voice softened. "Soldiers arrested them the day before yesterday, I am sorry to say. You will hear about it. Follow me. I have to hurry so I can return to my post."

The guard led them to a small settlement beside the river. His wife welcomed them into a stone hut, and he hurriedly explained why they had come.

"I have to go back to my post, Elba," he said.

"At least have a cup of tea to warm you. Sheep stealers will not be out on a cold night like this."

"I cannot take any chances. I will return home when the watch changes." He hurried out again.

Elba heated barley soup over a flickering fire in the center of the room. She seemed a kindly woman, and Segra took heart. "Please, tell me what you know about my parents," she begged.

"The day before yesterday, two soldiers came and asked for Garsil and Nalane. We were frightened. We had never seen soldiers in the valley before."

"Why did the soldiers want my parents?" Segra asked anxiously.

"Garsil inquired about that. He declared he would not go with them unless they told him why. The soldiers said that their orders were to bring them to the city of Molter, and that they had better start marching." Elba paused. "The soldiers were very rude, and they were armed with sharp spears."

"I wonder where they took them in Molter," Segra murmured.

"The soldiers did not say." Elba gave her a sympathetic smile. "I know your parents did not commit any crime. You could not find two kinder people. Garsil knew about medicine, and he was always helping people." She dished up bowls of soup and handed them to Brill and Segra.

Segra ate silently, but after a few minutes, Brill asked, "Did you know King Talder is back on the throne?"

"No!" exclaimed Elba. "That is wonderful news. If Immane is gone, we can go home again. We have not felt welcome here. The Magrans complain that our sheep are eating grass that belongs to their sheep. But there is no shortage of grass."

"Do you know if King Talder's son, Prince Silgar, is among the settlers here?" Brill asked.

She shook her head. "No, nobody by that name lives here."

"Are there other settlements of Exitornian exiles?" asked Brill.

"There might be. We do not get much news from other places," answered Elba.

That night, Brill and Segra slept in the stone hut. The next morning, they met with the rest of the villagers in front of the huts. Sheep huddled in wooden pens built against a rocky cliff.

"It is too cold to take our sheep to the mountain meadows now," explained one of the men.

"Please, give us the news from Exitorn," said a woman.

Brill described how Immane had been deposed and King Talder returned to the throne.

The small group raised a cheer at the news.

Once again, Brill asked, "Does anyone know if King Talder's son is in Magra?"

They whispered among themselves. One man spoke up, "We have not heard anything about the prince of Exitorn. Why are you asking?"

"He is missing—at least he was, the last I knew," answered Brill.

"We are sorry to hear that. I hope they find him soon." The leader motioned for the whisperers to listen. "Let us make plans to return home as soon as we can sell our sheep." He put a hand on Brill's shoulder. "Thank you for bringing us the news about King Talder. We hope to travel to the capital in a few days. Would you like to go with us?"

"Thank you," Segra answered, "but we have to get to Molter as fast as we can—in case Father and Mother move to another place."

The villagers wished them well. After thanking them, Brill and Segra started down the trail.

"It does not sound as if the prince is here in Magra, does it?" said Segra. "Perhaps he has been found and is back at the palace of Exitorn by now."

"I hope so. At least we know your parents are probably in Molter."

"But where are they in Molter? Why were they arrested? What can we do about it?" All the way down the rocky trail, Segra struggled with the endless questions in her mind.

By late afternoon, dark clouds hung low, and snowflakes began to drift down. Segra shivered. "We will not be able to sleep outside tonight."

"Not unless we want to turn into icicles." Brill looked at the map Vorn had given him. "We will soon be getting to the town of Wipet. Perhaps we can find an inn there."

"What will we use for money?"

"You still have your jewels, do you not?"

"Yes, but I know you do not want me to use them."

Brill sighed. "We have no choice. How else can we pay for shelter tonight?"

"I hate giving an expensive jewel for a night's lodging, but we cannot expect a Magran to open his home to us," Segra said. "It is clear that they do not like strangers."

At Wipet, they found an inn on the main street, but when Brill asked for lodging, the innkeeper looked at him suspiciously. "Let me see your money."

Segra showed him a small emerald. "I hate to give this up, but we need shelter tonight."

The man snatched at the emerald. "Pick out a straw mattress. I will even include a hot meal for both of you."

"Do you have a private room for the lady?" asked Brill.

The innkeeper scowled. "She is not dressed like a lady. She will have to sleep in the main hall like everyone else."

"That is fine." Segra did not want to cause any commotion that would draw attention to them.

They stood in a line and received bowls of watery stew. After eating, they laid their straw mattresses in a corner of the room. At least they were as far as possible from the long table where drinks and food were served.

The men at the inn preferred drinking to sleeping, and even after the innkeeper blew out the candles, they continued singing, arguing, and laughing. Segra lay awake for a long time, thinking about her parents.

She was awakened the next morning by a rough hand on her shoulder. "Where are the rest of the jewels?" demanded a cold voice. The soldier wore a dark orange uniform with gold fringe at his neck and on the bottom of his tunic. He must be one of the king's officers, Segra thought.

"What are you talking about?" She sat up slowly, not wanting to answer his question.

"Are you going to give them to me," he growled, "or do I have to search you?"

Brill jumped up. "Wait! You have no right—"

The officer drew himself up and glared at Brill. "Stand still or you die." He motioned to the other soldier beside him. "Hold her while I search."

"Yes, sir." The soldier bent over Segra, but she squirmed away and scrambled to her feet.

"They are my jewels, but I will give them to you."

She handed the sack to the officer, and he ripped it open. "Where did you get these?" he demanded.

She lifted her chin. "I was companion to the princess of Exitorn. She gave me a dress with the gems sewn to it."

"You are lying," he snapped. "These gems were stolen from the palace at Molter." As he spoke, the other soldier searched Brill and their belongings.

"I have never been to the king's palace," Segra insisted.

"You are going there now," said the officer grimly. "There is a room all ready for you. The king does not like people to steal his jewels."

"Let Brill go," Segra protested. "He has nothing to do with my jewels."

The officer did not answer. He dragged them to a cart outside and hurried them into it. The innkeeper rushed up. "You will not forget my reward? The king promised a reward for whoever found the jewel thieves."

The officer climbed into the cart. "I will give your name to my commander."

"I have friends in high places. You will be sorry if you try to claim the reward for yourself," cried the innkeeper.

The officer laughed as he nudged his companion. "Head for the palace."

The soldier raised his whip, and the horses pulled the cart down the icy road. "At least we do not have to walk," whispered Brill.

Segra's empty stomach lurched as the cart hit a hole. She tried to fight her despair. What was the penalty for stealing from the palace of Magra? In Exitorn, a person would be executed for doing such a thing.

9
The Royal Jewels

The box-shaped cart was meant for cargo, not human comfort, Segra decided. She and Brill clung to the sides as it skidded and bounced over the rough road.

Segra twisted her wrists inside the ropes until the skin felt rubbed off, but finally she could reach the knots and untie them. Quickly, she untied Brill's wrists, too.

"Thank you. That feels better," he whispered. "But we had better keep our wrists together if the soldiers look at us."

She nodded. Then she looked up at the gray clouds and nudged Brill. "I see a white bird."

"Where?"

"Above that hill." She sighed. "It might be Stargull. Oh, Brill, do you suppose he has been following us?"

"I have not seen him."

"But we have not looked. Maybe he has been keeping track of us."

Brill squinted at the sky. "That bird is too high to tell what it is."

Segra stared upward until her eyes watered. "I think I see the silver on his wings."

As the cart entered the capital city, Segra got to her knees. Crowds of people stood on either side of the road.

"What is going on?" she called to the officer.

"Festival Day. King Gabron will ride along the main road while the people cheer. Today he has Prince Silgar of Exitorn with him, and people are curious to see him."

"What?" Brill jumped up. "Have they found the lost prince?"

The officer did not turn around. "That is what they say."

"Where—where did they find him?" asked Brill.

The officer shrugged. "Somewhere in Magra. They say he was hiding from the emperor of Exitorn."

"That is wonderful news," murmured Segra.

"Now we will not have to search for the prince," Brill whispered. "As soon as we get back to Exitorn, I can go home."

Segra nodded. She wanted to point out that it might be a long time before they were free to return home. And she did not have a home until she could find her parents.

The cart passed under the arch of a thick wall that surrounded the palace grounds. Segra shivered as she looked up at the sharp spikes of the metal portcullis. She would not want to be underneath when that spiked gate fell. It was meant to seal the grounds from invaders, but she did not want to be sealed inside.

Soldiers stood at attention on either side of the road leading to the gray stone castle. It was such a tangle of rectangular buildings and tall, round towers that Segra wondered how people found their way around inside.

A soldier motioned to their driver. "Move your cart out of the way; here comes the king." The soldiers parted to let the driver guide the horses off the road.

"There is the king's carriage," said Brill. Segra craned her neck to see the prince.

King Gabron waved to the soldiers from his open gold coach. The man next to him was looking the other way, but then he turned. "Father!" Segra screamed. "Father—it is I!" She hoisted herself over the edge of the cart and prepared to jump.

"Stop her," yelled the officer.

A soldier prodded her back with his spear. "Where do you think you are going?"

"Please," she cried, "let me go to my father!"

Without answering, he pushed Segra down to the bottom of the cart. "Those two got their ropes off," he reported.

The officer turned and glared at her. "Nobody escapes from me. Stay down there or I will have you whipped."

"My father was sitting beside the king," whispered Segra. Why would the soldiers not believe her?

"Segra, are you sure?" asked Brill.

Segra swallowed. "I did not get a very good look at him. I want to see him so badly. Could I have imagined it?"

"Perhaps the man just looks like your father. It is not likely that a mountain doctor could really be a prince," pointed out Brill.

"But you said the prince was living among the common people so he would understand their problems."

"Surely he would have told his own daughter if he were a prince."

Segra sighed. "I suppose you are right. I feel rather faint, from not having breakfast, I think."

The driver halted the cart at a side door of the palace. Strong arms hustled Brill and Segra inside and down two flights of worn stone steps. As they came to a dark hall at the bottom, Segra began to cough. Musty, dank air filled her throat.

"Where are you, Meeg?" called the officer. "We have a couple of jewel thieves for you."

A fat, oily looking man emerged from the gloom. "Excellent! I have a fine place for these two. Bring them right along!"

Segra shuddered. They were shoved into a small cell, and the metal door closed behind them with an ominous clank.

Brill sat down on a cold stone bench. "Why do we always end up in dungeons?"

"I am sorry, Brill." Segra bit her lip to keep back the tears. "It is not fair that you should be locked up for trying to help me."

Brill stood up and began examining the damp stones that enclosed them. "We found a way out of that other dungeon. Perhaps we can do it again."

"We did not escape by ourselves—remember?"

"True." Brill sighed. "There is no one to help us here, and this cell seems to be well built."

"If they examine my jewels, they will realize they did not come from this palace."

"But surely you know that kings do not like unsolved crimes. They have to blame somebody."

"I keep thinking about the prince of Exitorn. His name is Silgar. My father's name is Garsil."

"So?" Brill gave her a puzzled glance.

"The syllables are reversed. Sil-gar—Gar-sil."

"You are right." He nodded. "Yes—that is strange."

Segra jumped to her feet and began to pace back and forth in the cell. "I am going to write the prince a letter."

"What are you going to use for paper, and how will you get it to him?" asked Brill.

She waved her hand, as if brushing away flies. "I have not worked out the details yet."

The door of the cell opened, and the jailer entered. Meeg handed each a bowl of green soup. Brill was hungry enough to lift the bowl to his mouth and take a big swallow. He choked. "This tastes like seaweed."

"Prisoners do not receive their food from the royal dining room," said Meeg. Then, to Segra's surprise, he asked, "How did you children manage to steal the royal jewels?"

"We did not steal any jewels from Magra," declared Segra.

He laughed. "Where did you steal them from?"

"The jewels are mine. I was the companion of the princess of Exitorn, and she gave them to me."

"If royalty hands out jewels to servants, Exitorn must have a good supply," said Meeg.

Brill put down his bowl of salty soup. "Emperor Immane liked jewels and gold. But he is not the ruler now."

Segra changed the subject. "Could I have a piece of paper and pen and ink?"

"Feel like writing a confession?" Meeg asked.

"I would like to write the truth," said Segra.

He nodded. "I can get you paper. Tell me about Exitorn. Where did Emperor Immane keep his jewels?"

"He never told us," answered Brill.

The jailer left, and the guards locked the cell door. Brill looked at Segra. "Why was he asking about Exitorn?"

"I have no idea. Maybe he is the jewel thief and plans to move to Exitorn to look for more gems."

"I do not like him," said Brill.

"I do not either, but we had better try to stay on the good side of him."

When Meeg returned to pick up their bowls, he handed Segra a small sheet of rough paper, a quill pen, and a horn of ink. "I am glad to be helpful," he said with a greasy smile.

Segra sat on the floor by the stone bench and thought how best to ask for the prince's help. She decided not to claim to be his daughter, for if she were wrong, that might anger him. She would just tell what she knew was the truth. She began her letter.

Dear Prince Silgar,

I am in prison for stealing gems, but I did not steal them. I was Princess Florette's companion in Exitorn, and she gave me the jewels. I am a friend of your father, King Talder, and I helped him to escape from prison and regain his throne. Please come to see me in the dungeon under the palace.

Your humble servant,

Segra

Brill read it when she finished. "I hope he can help us."

That night, as Segra lay sleepless on the cold stone floor, she kept repeating the names. "Silgar—Garsil." That could not be a coincidence. Garsil must be Prince Silgar. How could she ever get anyone to believe her?

The next morning when Meeg came with their thin gruel, Segra asked, "Could you please send someone to Prince Silgar of Exitorn with a letter?"

"Oh, so that is why you wanted paper." He shook his head. "Those of us who guard prisoners are not on friendly terms with the royal people who live above."

"But can you not find someone to deliver my letter?"

"Impossible! I try to be friendly to my prisoners and next thing you know they want me to traipse upstairs with their letters. Forget it." He stomped off, slamming the heavy door behind him.

"I am sorry your idea did not work," said Brill.

Segra wished she had one jewel left. She was sure Meeg would do anything for a price.

That afternoon as Meeg passed their cell, he called, "I am sorry to be the bearer of bad tidings, but your execution is scheduled for tomorrow."

"We are innocent!" cried Segra.

Meeg did not answer.

Segra tried to think. There was so little time. If the prince was her father, he would figure out a way to rescue them. She had to get that letter to him.

"Brill, I have to talk to Meeg."

"I do not think he will help us."

"He has to. He is the only one we can talk to."
Segra stood near the barred window and shouted,
"Meeg, Meeg! Come quick!"

He shuffled over to their cell. "What is the matter
now?"

"Meeg, this letter must go to Prince Silgar. He is
my father."

He snorted. "You have a wild imagination, girl."

"We came to Magra to find him. Oh, please,
Meeg, deliver my letter. When King Gabron hears I
have been wrongly accused, I am sure he will return
my jewels."

Meeg suddenly looked interested. "Are you of-
fering to pay me?"

"When I get my jewels back, I will give you a
large ruby."

"But if you do not get your jewels, I will not get
anything."

"Meeg, my father will see that you are rewarded
for saving my life."

Segra held the letter between the bars, and finally
Meeg took it. "I do know a maid upstairs who might
deliver it, but I will have to give her a jewel too."

"Of course. I will give you two rubies."

Meeg left with the letter.

"When Prince Silgar receives my letter, he will help us." Segra tried to sound brave.

Brill paced up and down the small square cell. "Even if the prince gets your letter, he does not have any power here in Magra."

"At least he can talk to King Gabron. All we can do is wait."

"I never was very good at waiting," Brill said with a sigh.

The time dragged by. Segra's hopes began to fade. If the prince had received her letter and wanted to help, he would be here by now.

"Must be supper time," said Brill as they heard the key turn in the door.

But it was not the jailer who entered. It was Prince Silgar. Dressed in a velvet, fur-trimmed tunic, he peered into the dimly lit cell. "Segra? Is there a girl called Segra here?"

Slowly, Segra stood up. "I am Segra," she answered in a trembling voice.

"Come closer so I can see you."

She took a step toward him. "My father's name was Garsil. Were you once called Garsil?"

"Yes, that was a name I used." His face lit up with joy. "Ah, yes! My child! I did not think I would ever see you again."

Segra threw herself into his arms. "Father, oh, Father! I have found you at last! I have been looking for you for such a long time."

From the doorway came Meeg's voice. "I knew these fine children could not be thieves."

Segra pulled away from her father. "Here, Father, this is Brill. He helped me look for you."

The prince shook his hand. "Thank you for taking care of my daughter, Brill."

"Everyone in Exitorn will rejoice to know that the lost prince is found," said Brill.

"Oh! What about Mother?" asked Segra. "Is she with you?"

"Yes. We will go to our room right now."

A servant approached and handed Segra her sack of jewels. "Your jewels are being returned by orders of King Gabron," he mumbled.

"Thank you," Segra replied. She pulled two rubies from the sack and gave them to Meeg. "Thank you for helping us."

Meeg smiled in his oily way as he looked at the glittering stones in his hand.

Segra and Brill followed her father up the stone stairs, past the great hall, and up another flight. He stopped in front of a large carved door. "Your mother does not know I found you. She was with the queen when I received your letter."

The prince opened the door and entered. His wife was sitting on a chair combing her long blond hair.

"Silgar, we are due in the great hall—" She turned and stared at Segra. She dropped her silver comb.

"I have found our daughter," said Silgar.

Segra's mother rose to her feet. She spoke hesitantly, as if she could hardly believe her eyes. "Segra! You have grown so tall—since I last saw you—so long ago. But your blue eyes and bright smile are the same."

"She is just as beautiful as her mother," said Prince Silgar.

The princess rushed to Segra and hugged her. Tears streamed down her cheeks. "We thought you were dead. That is why I could hardly let myself believe you were real."

Now Segra's tears came too. "I am so glad to be here. So glad!"

She looked up and saw Brill standing awkwardly in the doorway. "Brill, come and meet Mother." She took his hand. "Brill is my best friend, Mother, and he helped me to find you."

They all sat down, and Segra and Brill told her parents how they had helped to overthrow Emperor Immane's kingdom.

"I am proud of you both," said Prince Silgar.

Then Segra turned her attention to more practical matters. "Is there some way I can take a bath and wash my hair?"

"I will order a servant to fill the bathing tub," said her mother.

As a loud gong sounded, Silgar said, "I sent word to the king that we would not be at dinner tonight. I have ordered food for us to eat here, Nalane."

"How wonderful," said his wife with a contented smile. "It would be hard to listen to one of King Gabron's self-centered monologues tonight."

The prince nodded. "It is important for us to spend time together. After I received Segra's letter, I protested to King Gabron. I asked why an Exitornian with the same name as my daughter had been arrested. And no one had even thought to compare the jewels!"

"What did he say?" asked Segra.

"He blamed a servant for the mistake, and he ordered the jewels returned to you. But I still mistrust him."

A servant entered to fill the wooden tub in the small adjoining room. When her bath was ready, Segra left the others.

The warm water relaxed her tired muscles, and she leaned back into it with a happy sigh. Finally she gave her hair a final rinse and stepped from the tub. A servant had pressed the pink dress trimmed with lace that Florette had given her, and she put it on. When she rejoined the others, she saw that Brill too had bathed and was wearing a borrowed blue tunic with white hose. He bowed as Segra entered. "Your humble servant, my lady."

"Do not be silly."

"I am not being silly, Segra. You are from a royal family. Your friends will not be shepherds like me."

She smiled. "I will choose whom I want for my friends, and you will always be my best friend."

Brill nodded. "We have gone through a lot together."

They joined Segra's parents, who were sitting around a table in the large room. A servant served their dinner from the palace kitchen—roast chicken, sliced beef in a savory sauce, vegetables, rolls, and berriball cakes.

"This is the best meal we have had since we lived in the palace at Exitorn," exclaimed Brill.

Segra nodded. Never again would she have to eat prison gruel or chew on stale black bread. Best of all, her family was all together again.

"Father," she asked, "why did you not tell me you were a prince?"

He smiled. "You were only a child. I was afraid you might tell one of your friends and the news would spread. Think of the danger to us if any of Immane's spies had found out that King Talder's son still lived."

"You were right," she said. "If I had known I was a princess, I might have been tempted to share the secret."

"Now let us hear how you got to Magra," said the prince.

Segra and Brill took turns telling the tale. After they finished, Segra said, "Let us hurry back to Exitorn."

Prince Silgar frowned. "It is not quite that simple, my dear. King Gabron keeps delaying our departure. He keeps saying that he wants us to stay a little longer. He is up to something, but I do not know what."

10
Too Dangerous

Segra and Brill said good night and went to their assigned rooms. As Segra climbed onto the bed and sank into its soft mattress, she thought of all the uncomfortable places she had slept in during the past few weeks.

She heard a knock at the door. "Come in," she called.

Her mother opened her door. "Are you comfortable?"

"Oh, yes, thank you." Her mother came close to the bed and smoothed Segra's hair back from her face. "I can hardly believe I have you back, my child."

Segra sat up and hugged her. "Tell me a story? Like you used to?"

"Ah, yes, those were happy times, were they not?" Her mother sat down near the bed. "What shall I tell you?"

"You never would say how you met Father—and now I know why," said Segra. "Will you tell me all about it?" She settled herself against the pillows as her mother smiled and began the tale.

"Your father disguised himself and traveled through Exitorn to get to know the people, as you have heard. He loved the mountains and the mountain people, and finally he settled in the village of Trona. He had studied medicine with the palace doctor, and he became well loved because of his medical skill. He used the name Garsil. No one dreamed he was a prince."

"Did you live in that village?" asked Segra.

"Yes. My father was a goatherd. One day he was caught in an avalanche and broke his leg. Garsil set the bone, and then he herded our goats while my father's leg mended. I helped him, as I had my father."

"And he fell in love with you."

"I guess he did, although he did not say anything. He was the kindest man I had ever met, and I loved him with all my heart. When Father could herd the goats once more, Garsil went away. My heart broke. I later learned he had returned to the palace to tell his father that he wanted to marry me and live in the village for a few more years. King Talder argued against the plan, but finally he agreed."

Segra sighed. "It is such a romantic story."

"I was overjoyed when Garsil returned. He asked me to marry him, and of course I said yes. Then he told me who he really was, and I was shocked and scared. I did not know anything about being a princess. I married him anyway, and we were very happy. Garsil and I were planning to move to the palace when Immane became ruler."

"Did Father ever think of raising an army so he could rescue his father and overthrow Immane?"

"He thought about it a great deal. When Immane took over the kingdom, we fled to a settlement even higher in the mountains. You were only two years old then. Garsil and a group of men met secretly to plan a way to overthrow Immane, but it was very difficult to buy weapons, and it was impossible to train an army of any size with Immane's spies everywhere."

Segra's mother stared into the distance, and then she rose, as if to leave.

"Do not go yet," said Segra.

"But you must be very tired. You need to sleep."

Segra pushed the covers aside, jumped up, and hugged her mother. "I am glad you told me about meeting Father. But I want to know how King Gabron found you."

"Apparently King Talder learned that we had gone to Magra, and he sent a messenger to find your father. The messenger was intercepted by Magran soldiers who brought him to the palace. King Gabron read the message addressed to your father and then ordered soldiers to search for a man named Garsil. Eventually they found us, and King Gabron asked your father many questions. When he was satisfied that Garsil really was the prince, he entertained us with a lavish banquet. He says he wants to be friends with the future king of Exitorn."

"But Father does not trust him, does he?"

"No. The king keeps delaying our departure. The messenger from Exitorn is being kept at the palace, too. Gabron talks about sending him to King Talder someday soon. But your father says he does not need anyone to say he is coming—he just wants to go."

"Could we just slip away?"

"The palace is surrounded by a high wall and is well guarded. We cannot leave until King Gabron allows us to go."

Segra climbed back into bed. "There must be some way to get out."

Her mother tucked her in. "Ah, Segra, you always were impatient. We must wait until the time is right." She leaned over and kissed her good night. "It is so wonderful to have you with us again. Let us enjoy this time and not worry about King Gabron."

The next evening King Gabron invited them to a banquet celebrating Segra's reunion with her parents. The long table was piled high with food.

King Gabron leaned toward Segra. "Are you enjoying the party, little princess?"

"Very much, thank you," she answered. The king was a tall lean man with a narrow face. His black eyes darted about. "The windows of a crafty brain," she thought, remembering that description from a book she had read.

A wandering minstrel sang and told stories after dinner. He fought imaginary beasts with an imaginary sword. Then a group of acrobats performed a funny routine.

Segra's mother whispered to her between the performances. "The lady next to me says the thief who stole the palace jewels has been discovered."

"Who?"

"The jailer—his name was Meeg. Did you meet him?"

"Oh, yes. Have they locked him up?"

"Not yet. He ran away before they could catch him."

When they returned to their rooms, Segra asked, "Father, did you ask the king about going home?"

"I asked. He said that storms are keeping the ships in port."

"That is ridiculous," said Brill. "Segra and I climbed one of the towers today. The sky was blue, and ships were sailing back and forth. The wind was strong, but the sea was not stormy."

Prince Silgar looked grave. "The king always has some excuse. I do not understand why he wants to keep us here."

The next day, the messenger from Exitorn burst into their room. "Today I am being sent back to Exitorn with a letter for King Talder," he announced.

"We will all go with you," Prince Silgar said firmly. "I will speak to Gabron at once."

Segra looked at her father with admiration. He would be able to convince King Gabron that they must leave.

But when he returned, his face was taut with anger. "Gabron has revealed his evil plan."

"What happened?" cried Segra's mother.

"We are prisoners."

"What do you mean?" Segra ran to her father.

"Soldiers followed me when I left the throne room. They stand outside our door right now."

Segra's mother frowned. "King Gabron said we were his guests."

"Not any longer. Actually I am the only one who is a prisoner. King Gabron is demanding that my father give him Velvet Valley in exchange for me. But my father will never agree to give up land where our people have lived for centuries."

"If King Talder does not agree, what will happen to you?" Segra's mother clasped her hands together.

"Gabron says I will die, but I do not believe him."

Segra put her arm around her mother. "We must find a way to escape."

"Gabron will pay for such treachery," said the prince in a low voice.

"Let us go for a walk, Segra," said Brill. She nodded and followed him.

Two soldiers stood on each side of the door. They did not question Segra and Brill, but she felt sure her father could not leave his room without an armed escort.

They climbed the wedge-shaped stairs of the nearest tower. As they reached the top, they looked out over the harbor and the city. The towers on the city wall were manned by soldiers, but the castle towers were not.

Segra leaned against the stone battlements, determined to find a way for her father to escape. Finally she said, "Brill, you might be able to go home with the messenger."

"I will not leave you—not until you are safe in Exitorn."

"But it is not fair that you are spending so much time on my problems."

"I am serving my country when I serve its princess," he said in a quiet voice.

Segra smiled. "Thank you, Brill. Between us perhaps we can think of a plan to help Father. But the only door is guarded by soldiers, and the arrow slits are too narrow to climb through."

"Perhaps the soldiers will fall asleep at night."

Segra looked thoughtful. "But even if we got away from the guards, how would we get beyond the city walls? Soldiers are everywhere. I hope Grandfather will know how to bring Father and us home again."

Two weeks later, King Gabron received an answer to his message. He called Prince Silgar and his family to the great hall. A dozen richly dressed nobles were sitting before the throne, as if they had been consulting with the king.

Segra tried to read the expression on Gabron's face. He scowled in anger, but his black eyes shone.

He glared at Prince Silgar. "Apparently you do not mean much to your father." Gabron read from King Talder's letter. *I will not sacrifice my country's land, even for my son. Release him at once, or I shall take military action.*

Prince Silgar stared back at the king. "I told you my father would never give up our people's land."

Segra was proud of her father's erect posture and firm voice.

"You were right." Gabron smiled, and his voice took on a pleasant tone. "I shall have to change the terms of your release." He cleared his throat, and Segra wondered why he looked so pleased. "Many years ago, Khalom, a tribal chief in Asperita, stole the ancient jeweled crown of Magra. It bears the famous diamond of Magra and is of great sentimental value as well. I have decided that I will set you free if you can get the crown back."

"I have heard the story of your stolen crown," Prince Silgar said. He added thoughtfully, "You have no right to require this of me, but I will help you to find it. I shall leave at once for Asperita."

Gabron laughed. "Ah, it would not be smart to let you leave, my fine prince. Do you take me for a fool? Of course you would escape."

The prince gave him a level glance. "My word, unlike yours, Gabron, can be trusted. I cannot find the crown from my guarded room."

Gabron flushed angrily. "I suggest that you write to your father. I am sure he will have an idea how to get my crown. His messenger can take the letter back with him. Now get out of my sight."

Back in their room, Prince Silgar sank down on a chair. "Gabron has figured out a new way to get Velvet Valley."

"What do you mean?" asked Segra.

"If my father sends soldiers to Asperita to recover the crown, the Asperitans will attack Exitorn. Then Gabron will march into Velvet Valley. Exitorn is not strong enough to fight both Asperita and Magra at the same time."

"Your father is wise. He will know what to do." Segra's mother put an arm around her husband.

"I am not going to write to my father about the crown," he said.

"But you must tell him. That is our only hope!" she cried.

"I will write that we are doing well and not to worry. I will not have Exitorn go to war because of me. My life is not that important."

"It is to me!" she exclaimed.

Prince Silgar shrugged. "Gabron would not dare to kill me. Eventually he will get tired of his game and let me go."

"Father, do you know what the crown looks like?" asked Segra.

"I have heard that it is made from a rare, light-weight metal called zalium. It has a wonderful silver sheen. Besides containing the great diamond of Magra, the crown is set with many priceless gems."

"I would like to see it," said Segra. "Brill, shall we walk up to the tower?"

When they reached the top, Segra said, "Lopet's father promised he would do anything for us. Perhaps we can ask him to take us to Asperita in his boat."

Brill's eyes widened. "There is no way you can get the crown. I have heard about the cruelty of the Asperitans."

"I have a plan. Somehow we will get to where that tribal chief lives. What is his name—?"

"Khalom," said Brill.

"Yes, Khalom. And we will find out where he keeps the crown and when he wears it. Then I will ask Stargull to quickly fly over and grab it off his head."

Brill grimaced. "Becoming a princess has addled your brain. This is your wildest idea yet."

She ignored Brill's objections. "First we will go to Pover to find Stargull."

"How do you know he is on Pover?"

"I have not seen Stargull since that day we entered the palace. I think he lives on Pover."

"Even if we find him, how do you know he will understand you?"

"Because he is very intelligent. He is our best chance to recover the stolen crown."

Brill sighed. "This idea is too dangerous, Segra. Let us think of something else."

"You do not have to come with me. I will do it alone," Segra declared.

"No, I will not let you go alone." He took a deep breath. "You will need help."

11

At Sea Again

The next day as Segra and Brill hurried to Lopet's home, Brill said, "I fear that Asperita is a dangerous place."

"If we can find Stargull, my plan will work."

"You are brave, Segra, but this time you may be trying to do the impossible."

Segra knocked on Lopet's door. When he saw them, the boy squealed with happiness.

Vorn rubbed his chin nervously as he listened to Segra's plan. "I promised I would do anything for you, and I will keep my word," he said slowly. "Getting to Pover will not be a problem except for the current in the strait, but I do not like the thought of sailing to Asperita."

"You do not have to stay. Just drop us off," said Segra.

"And pick us up again," added Brill.

"The Asperitans have the reputation of thinking only of themselves. They have been known to kidnap foreigners to use as slaves. They enslave their own people too, if they cannot pay their debts," warned Vorn.

"We will be careful," promised Segra.

"Can I go too?" begged Lopet.

Vorn frowned. "I need another rower in case we do not get enough wind, but you are too small to be much help, son."

"I can row," offered Brill. "Segra and I rowed across the current that runs past Pover."

"I can bail," cried Lopet.

His father patted his head. "All right, son, you may come." He looked at Brill and Segra. "Be here early tomorrow morning."

They nodded and said good-bye. Before they returned to the palace, Segra sold the rest of her jewels, thinking that coins would be less conspicuous for buying what they needed. She was surprised at how much money the larger jewels brought—over a hundred gold half-coins as well as some silver.

That evening they told Segra's parents that they would like to take a trip with Lopet and his father.

Segra's mother frowned. "Why do you want to go sailing after your terrible shipwreck?"

"We will be safe, Mother. Vorn goes fishing all the time and nothing has happened to him."

"Vorn and Lopet are our friends," Brill added. "It will be fun to spend some time with them."

Segra's mother sighed. "I do not blame you. It is difficult to sit and wait for whatever Gabron will think up next."

The following day was clear and cold. The sail of Vorn's small fishing boat billowed out in the brisk wind as they skimmed across the water. Vorn steered with an oar while Brill, Segra, and Lopet watched for rocks. It was almost dark when they slipped into the cove on Pover and dropped anchor.

"We will wait until morning to go ashore," said Vorn.

Segra longed to see Florette. She looked toward the hill where the former royal family lived. "Brill, why is there no smoke coming from the chimney?"

"I have been wondering the same thing. I do not see Stargull either."

"He may be sleeping."

They helped Vorn prepare a meal, then ate in silence—except for Lopet, who kept up a constant chatter. That night they snuggled under layers of fur, but the icy chill slipped beneath their covers.

At dawn, they arose stiff and cold. Segra jumped up and down to help her blood circulate.

Vorn and Brill rowed the boat to shore. While they were hauling it up onto the beach, Segra ran up the path. She knocked on the door of the house, but there was no answer. She pushed the door open and looked around.

"No one is here," she reported to Brill as he entered the house.

"A ship must have picked them up," said Brill. "You had better start looking for your bird. That is what we came for." He turned and left the small house.

"I thought Stargull would see me by now."

"I hope Grossder did not shoot him after we left."

"Stargull is too smart for that." Segra ran along the path to the cliff where Stargull had picked the glondine for her. Brill followed at a slower pace.

"Stargull," she called. Her eyes searched the windswept pines at the top of the cliff. She saw a few seagulls flying above her, but nothing as large as the meladora bird. Her plan would not work without Stargull! What if he had returned to the far-off land where the meladoras lived? She tried to push the worries from her mind.

Finally, Brill said, "If we cannot find the bird, let us go to Exitorn and tell King Talder about the crown."

"No!" Segra looked at him in alarm. "Father does not want King Talder to fight Asperita—not even to save his life."

"Your father is very brave," Brill said with a smile. "You must have inherited your courage from him."

"I do not feel very brave now. I need Stargull so much." Again she called, "Stargull! Stargull, oh, please come back!"

She heard his deep cry before she saw the great bird swoop down toward her. He landed at her feet and folded his wings close to his body.

Segra sat down beside him, stroking his silver-tipped feathers. He cocked his head as she explained the mission. "You are the only one who can help us," she said.

He made a guttural sound as if in answer, and Segra wished she understood his language.

She stood, motioning for Stargull to follow. She and Brill ran to the beach where Vorn and Lopet were cooking fresh fish.

"This smells wonderful," said Segra. The delicately browned fish and hearty bread soon satisfied their hunger. Segra fed Stargull a piece of raw fish.

"If you feed him, he may come along just for the fish," Brill said. "We will not know whether he understands his mission."

"He understands," Segra insisted.

"I have never seen a bird like this before," said Vorn. "Much too big for a gull. I wonder what kind it is."

"He is a meladora bird," said Lopet. "Do you not remember the stories Grandmother told about meladora birds?"

"Yes, Lopet, but I thought they had disappeared long ago." Vorn studied the huge bird. He said slowly, "This bird does look like the ones your grandmother described."

After breakfast they began their journey to Asperita. When the wind was calm, they rowed. The boat was big for two rowers, so they made slow progress. When the wind blew, they hoisted the sail and made better time. At night Stargull perched on deck to sleep. In the daytime Segra often saw him soaring high above the boat. He did not have to flap his wings when he was riding the air currents.

Brill liked to look over Vorn's shoulder when he was studying the map to identify the land they were passing. Vorn said, "It has been many years since my last trip to Asperita."

After several days at sea, Vorn steered the boat into the harbor of Asperita's capital.

"I will be fishing in these waters and trying to sell my fish in the marketplace," he said. "Look for me when you are ready to go home."

"Thank you for bringing us here," said Segra.

"I just hope you do not get into trouble. Asperita has many nomads who travel with their flocks," he warned. "Some of them are fierce fighters. Be careful who you talk to."

"We will," promised Segra. She and Brill scrambled off the boat and hurried to buy supplies in the marketplace.

"How are you going to find out where Chief Khalom and his crown are?" asked Brill.

"We will need a guide."

Brill looked around. "Who can we trust?"

"We will find someone," said Segra.

"I have not seen Stargull today."

Segra looked up at the sky. "We do not always see him. But I am sure he flies high and checks on us."

Colorfully dressed people crowded the marketplace. Segra bought bread, dried beef strips, and nuts. They stopped at a booth where savory chicken pieces were cooking over an open fire. After some discussion about the price, they bought two pieces and sat down in a doorway to eat.

"Brill, there is a slave market." Segra pointed to a platform where several people were chained to a wooden railing. She watched as the spectators bid on a brawny young man.

"Look at these muscles!" cried the auctioneer.

Soon the young slave was led away by his purchaser.

"Let us go," urged Brill. "We need to find a place to camp tonight."

But Segra did not move. The next slave to be sold was a girl about her age. Her long black hair fell limply around her thin shoulders. Her dull eyes reflected the misery of her life.

Segra stood, then edged toward the crowd.

"Where are you going?" asked Brill.

"Beautiful slave girl," the auctioneer called. "Perfect health. Willing worker. What am I bid?"

"Ten half-coins," called a plump man. Segra glanced at him. His eyes looked cruel. She hoped he would not buy the girl.

Another man bid fifteen half-coins, and the bids went back and forth until the second man dropped out.

The cruel man was buying the girl for thirty gold half-coins.

"Thirty-five," called Segra.

"Are you out of your mind?" whispered Brill.

"Forty." The man scowled at Segra.

"Forty-five," said Segra.

"Fifty. My final bid."

"Fifty-five," said Segra.

"Sold," cried the auctioneer.

"Segra, what have you done?" asked Brill.

"I could not let that cruel man have her."

Brill sighed. "I guess she could be our guide, but we do not even know if she knows the country very well."

Segra walked up to the platform and counted out the money. The girl looked at her in surprise.

"Take off the chain," ordered Segra.

"You can take it off when you get out of the city. Otherwise she may run off," advised the auctioneer.

"I want it off now."

The auctioneer motioned to an assistant, and he sawed off the chain that held the girl's wrists together.

"What is your name?" asked Segra.

"Rima." She still looked astonished.

"Do you know the way through the city?" asked Segra.

Rima nodded.

They left the slave auction with Rima leading them through the crowded marketplace. Then they walked through a maze of narrow streets where ragged children stood staring at them from the open doorways of small, one-story clay houses.

Brill caught up with Segra. "Two men are following us."

"Are you sure?"

"Very sure. Every time we turn, they do too."

Rima looked back. "Those are Omed's men."

"Who is Omed?" asked Segra.

"The man you bid against. I am afraid he let you buy me with the idea of capturing all of us—thereby getting three slaves without spending any money."

"Run!" Segra cried. "We have to lose them. Rima, what is the best way to go?"

"Follow me," she said. The three sprinted away as fast as they could, darting through narrow alleys and along streets where they dodged donkey carts and camels.

"I think we have lost them," gasped Brill.

Rima slowed up a little. "Do you know where a chieftain named Khalom lives?" Segra asked, after she had caught her breath.

"Why?" asked Rima.

"We need to see him."

"He lives in the South—a long way from here."

Segra thought fast. "Is there some place where we can buy horses?"

"I know a place near the edge of town. I can take you there if you like."

"Please do."

Rima led them down a dusty road where the houses were not so close together. They kept looking over their shoulders to make sure their pursuers were not trailing them.

"I think we have escaped Omed," said Segra.

"Keep watching. Omed never gives up." Rima pointed to a stable. "Let me do the bartering for the horses. How much can you spend?"

Segra thought about the money she had left. "Can we get horses for fifteen half-coins each?"

"I will try." Rima ran over to the horse dealer. She talked fast to the man, describing what they needed.

"Twenty gold half-coins for each horse," said the man.

"Ten," offered Rima.

"I have fine horses. I would not sell any of them for ten half-coins."

Rima raised her offer to twelve.

"Seventeen," countered the man.

"Fifteen," answered Rima. She looked at Segra with a question in her dark eyes as if to say, "Should I go higher?"

Brill nudged Segra. "Can you not hurry her? Those men could find us at any moment."

"I will tell her to hurry." Segra walked closer to Rima.

The man was grumbling about the price, but finally he said, "I will see what I can find for that price."

He walked inside the stable, and Segra whispered, "We need to get away from here."

Rima said, "I know our danger, but I am following your orders. It takes time to buy horses." Rima examined the horses as he brought each one out. "No, no, that one is too old," she declared when he showed her the last one.

"What do you expect for fifteen half-coins?" muttered the dealer.

"A horse that has a few good years left. Maybe we can do better at another stable."

The dealer scowled. "I will replace the last one. You will have three fine horses, but I hate to sell them for such a low price."

"Where are the saddles and bridles?" demanded Rima.

"That will be another half-coin for each."

"No, they should be included with the horses," said Rima.

Segra frowned. They needed to get away before Omed found them. She reached in her pouch to count out her coins.

By the time she had finished, the horse dealer had agreed to include used saddles and bridles.

Segra paid the man, and they mounted the horses. "Now we can travel fast and keep away from Omed's men," Segra said.

Rima led them away from the city and across the grassland. Only a few trees and shrubs dotted the plain. Segra kept looking back, but she saw no other riders. Her fears began to subside.

Rima's long black hair blew in the wind as she urged her horse toward the stone cliffs that rose in the distance.

As they drew near the cliffs, Segra saw that they formed a canyon. "Those men will not find us here," she called. Surely the walls of the canyon would hide them from view.

"Omed will not give up easily," warned Rima. "There are caves here if you want to camp overnight."

"That is a good plan," agreed Segra, "since it is beginning to get dark." She looked for Stargull, but she saw no sign of him in the sky overhead. She began to worry that the bird might not have followed them. Without Stargull, their plan would not work.

They found a large cave and tethered their horses next to a good supply of grass for grazing.

"Thank you, Rima, for guiding us out of the city and for buying the horses at such a good price," said Segra.

Rima looked at her. "Masters do not usually thank their slaves."

"When I took off your chains, I released you from slavery. Did you not understand that?"

Rima shook her head, looking at Segra as if she wondered whether her new owner was playing a joke on her.

"I only bought you to save you from Omed," Segra said.

"But why would you throw money away like that?" asked Rima.

"I could not let you be sold to a cruel man. Our Book of Wisdom says, *Kindness buys more lasting happiness than jewels.*"

"My life has not been easy," Rima said. "I do not expect good things to happen to me."

"I hope you will stay with us until we complete our mission."

Rima nodded. "I will help you in any way I can."

While they ate a cold supper, Segra explained their quest to find the stolen crown. Rima shook her head in disbelief. "It belongs to Chief Khalom, but there is no way you can steal it. When he is awake, he wears it. At night it is put in a locked box that is lowered into a pit of poisonous snakes. Armed guards stand around the pit."

"What does Khalom do to people who try to steal it?" Brill asked.

"He has them thrown into the pit of snakes," answered Rima. "Many in Asperita would like that crown, but no one has ever been able to take it from Khalom. There is a saying among the people that if Khalom ever loses the crown, he will also lose his throne. So he guards it closely."

"We have a plan," Segra assured her. "Do you know the way to Khalom's house?"

"Yes. He has a huge mansion about a day's journey from here."

"Will you lead us there?"

"Yes, but please do not order me to steal the crown. I do not want to be thrown into the snake pit."

"Just guide us to Khalom's house."

From where he leaned against a boulder, Brill said to Rima. "It sounds as if you know Asperita pretty well."

"My father was a trader, so I traveled with him. When he died, I was sold to help pay his debts."

"That is terrible," cried Segra.

"My father had enemies." Her voice trembled. "I have not been well treated."

"Did your father teach you how to bargain with horse dealers?"

Rima smiled. "My father said I was better than he was at buying horses. I miss him a great deal." She wiped her eyes on her sleeve.

The cave protected them from the wind, but it was damp. No matter how tightly Segra wrapped her cloak around herself, she could not get warm enough to sleep. "When I get back to the castle in Exitorn, I am never going to sleep outside again," she muttered.

At the first light of dawn, they arose, ate a quick breakfast, and mounted their horses. Segra watched the sky, hoping to see Stargull.

They had started across another flat plain when they noticed three horses fast approaching from the direction of the city they had left behind.

"I hope those are not Omed's men," exclaimed Rima.

"Can we go any faster?" asked Segra.

"At the price you paid, you did not get race horses," said Rima.

Rima glanced back. "It is Omed. I can see his bald head. Nothing can save us now."

At that moment Segra heard a harsh cry, and she looked up to see Stargull circling above them. "Stargull, can you help us?" she called.

"Who is Stargull?" asked Rima, looking around.

"Look up. He is a very large bird." Segra leaned close to her horse's neck, urging him to greater speed, but their pursuers were gaining on them and there was no place to hide.

"Our horses cannot outrun theirs," cried Rima.

Segra looked up at Stargull again. Could one bird fight Omed and his men?

The three horsemen galloped up to them. "You are my slaves—all of you," Omed shouted. "No one opposes Omed of Asperita!"

Stargull swooped down, nipping Omed's horse on the flank. The horse reared, throwing its rider to the ground.

Rima, Brill, and Segra galloped away while Omed's companions jumped off their horses to tend to him. "Where can we go?" called Segra.

"There are more rock canyons on the other side of the plains, but they are a long way off," answered

Rima. "I have never seen a bird that huge. Why did he attack Omed and not us?"

"He is a meladora bird—and our friend," said Segra.

"Omed is back on his horse," Brill said. "And they are coming after us again."

Segra looked back to see Stargull dive at the horsemen again, but this time a man shot an arrow toward him. Stargull flew higher. The element of surprise was gone, and whenever he dropped lower, arrows flew upward.

Omed and his men drew closer and closer. This time Segra knew Stargull could not help them without endangering his own life.

12

Where Is Stargull?

Segra urged her horse to go faster. Stargull flew ahead of them, dipping down close, then up again. "He wants us to follow," called Segra, catching up with Rima.

"He is only a brainless bird."

"Just follow him," said Segra.

Stargull led them to a wide river where several dinogators lay partly submerged. One lifted a scaly head and bellowed, showing sharp teeth.

"Dinogators!" cried Rima.

"They sound angry," said Brill.

Segra galloped ahead. "Come on! Stargull is leading us across the river."

"I do not want to be eaten by dinogators!" exclaimed Rima.

"Wait, Segra!" Brill shouted. "The dinogators of Asperita may not be as friendly as those in Exitorn."

"This is our only chance," Segra called. Her horse splashed into the river.

Brill followed her. The dinogators stayed in the middle of the river.

Rima plunged her horse into the water just as Omed and his men galloped to the riverbank.

"Come back," shouted Omed, "before the dinogators eat you!"

Segra bent low over her horse and pulled up her feet as it rode through the water. One dinogator opened its mouth and bellowed, but it made no move to attack.

"They are getting away. Let us go after them," called Omed.

"Not me," shouted one of his men. "My brother was bitten by a dinogator."

Another man called, "You had better not go either, Omed. The dinogators will not be able to resist a meaty fellow like you."

Omed shook his head. "We have wasted enough time chasing them. They would not make good slaves." He waved his men to follow him back toward the city.

Segra, Brill, and Rima stopped on the far bank. "Omed has turned back," cried Segra in delight.

"We were fortunate those dinogators were not hungry," said Rima in a trembling voice.

"Which way do we go?" asked Segra.

"We follow the river until we reach the bridge that leads across to the south lands," answered Rima. "Then we turn toward the sea."

"I am glad you know the country," said Segra. "Where is Chief Khalom's land?"

"Between the river and the sea," said Rima.

They resumed their journey at a more leisurely pace. Segra explained to Rima how she had met Stargull and how she hoped he could snatch the crown.

"It is difficult to believe that a bird can understand you, but perhaps it is true," said Rima. "Why were you not afraid of those fierce dinogators?"

Segra told her how she had made friends with the remarkable dinogator she had named Peachy, and how the dinogators had helped overthrow Emperor Immane.

Rima patted her horse. "Maybe animals are smarter than we think."

"I do not know if all dinogators are friendly to people," Segra said, "but the ones we have met have not eaten anyone."

"You heard Omed's man say his brother was bitten by one."

"Perhaps the brother injured one of them."

"Perhaps."

They passed several tent camps along the river.

"When will we come to the bridge?" asked Brill.

"Not until tomorrow," answered Rima.

That night Segra felt stiff and sore from riding all day, and she fell asleep almost right away.

The next morning they ate a simple breakfast and then rode for an hour before crossing back over the river on a wide wooden bridge.

"We are not far from Khalom's territory now," said Rima.

"Is his tribe friendly?" asked Segra.

"We Asperitans are not known for friendliness. I do not think Khalom's men will bother us as long as we are just passing through. But if the crown is stolen, the chieftain will suspect strangers."

The road wound up a rocky hill. From the top they looked down upon a town of gray houses with pink tile roofs. Rima pointed to a large two-story house surrounded by a high wall and colorful gardens. "That is where Khalom lives."

Beyond the city, they could see the sea.

Segra stared at the mansion. Was Chief Khalom there? Would he come out wearing his crown? Would Stargull be able to lift the crown and get away without being shot? She had not considered the danger to Stargull when she made her plans.

Segra turned to the others. "Let us find a place to meet in case we are separated."

Rima led the way down the hill, and they followed a narrow path to a beach that was covered with small rocks. Segra looked around and motioned toward a cave in the rocky cliff behind them. She walked closer to the cave and glanced into it. "This would be a good meeting place."

"Let us try not to get separated," said Brill.

"We probably will not, but we need a place for Stargull to find us." Segra looked up at Stargull, who had perched nearby. "Bring the crown to this cave, Stargull."

They rode back to the town and tethered their horses outside the city wall. The gates were open, but soldiers patrolled the city on horseback.

When they reached the gates of Khalom's estate, Rima said, "It is best to wait outside until he comes out."

Segra frowned. "That might take days."

"We must be patient." Rima sat in the shade of a bushy tree, and the others joined her. Stargull perched on a branch, hidden by the thick foliage.

Segra tried to relax, but every nerve was tingling for action.

Several hours later she jumped up as Khalom's gate swung open. Four soldiers rode out, followed by the chieftain astride a white horse. His jeweled crown sparkled in the sunlight.

Segra stood up. "There it is, Stargull," she whispered. "That is the crown we need."

The bird cocked his head and stared at Khalom.

Segra wondered if he was afraid, since Omed's arrows had so narrowly missed him. "Stargull, please try."

Stargull still watched as Khalom and his men passed by.

"I do not think Stargull understands what you want," said Rima.

"He understands," answered Segra. "I think he is afraid of the guards' arrows." She turned to Stargull, but he was gone.

In the next instant, the great meladora bird swooped down upon Khalom. He snatched the crown in his talons and rose high into the sky with a mighty beating of his silver-tipped wings.

"My crown!" shouted Khalom. "Help! Help!"

His guards raised their bows and shot dozens of arrows at the departing bird.

Segra watched as he climbed higher and higher, the crown reflecting the sun's rays in flashes of light. She breathed more easily as soon as he was safely out of range.

"Follow that bird," roared Khalom to his soldiers. They galloped down the main street toward the city gate.

"Alert more soldiers," he shouted to an officer. "Close the city gates! No one may leave except my men. Find out who is working with that bird."

"We must hide," Rima whispered.

Segra looked to see if anyone was watching them suspiciously, so close to Khalom's house, but everyone's attention was on the sky and the enraged chieftain. Now all they had to do was escape from the city, but it would not be easy.

She and Brill followed Rima back to the main part of town, and they paused behind a clump of bushes. "We should act as if we are just going about our daily activities," whispered Segra.

"Your blond hair makes you conspicuous," answered Rima. "Most Asperitans have darker coloring." She handed Segra a scarf. "Here—try to hide your hair. I should have thought of that sooner."

They stayed in the bushes while Segra tied the scarf around her head. Groups of soldiers were assembling in answer to the shouts of their leaders. One soldier yelled, "Hurry, we want someone from our troop to find the crown. Chief Khalom has promised a fine reward to the fortunate man and his troop."

Rima, Segra, and Brill started off again, but soon the street was filled with mounted soldiers, and they had to duck into a doorway. When they had ridden by, Rima led them to an alley and pushed open the door of a small cottage.

"Who lives here?" asked Segra, looking around the tidy little room.

"A woman who traded with my father. She must have gone on an errand, but I hope she will hide us until we can get out of the city."

"I am worried about Stargull." Segra frowned. "If he leaves the crown in that cave, will the soldiers see him and shoot him? Will they find the crown?"

"Stargull is smart," Brill said. "He will not leave the crown if he sees soldiers."

"I wish I could see what is happening."

"They will not let you through the gates without a lot of questioning," said Rima.

"I know. It is just so hard to wait, not knowing what is going on."

"Try to calm down, Segra," Brill said. "We do not want to fall into Khalom's hands."

"We must stay here until we find a safe way to leave the city," added Rima.

The owner of the house finally came home. She looked frightened when Rima asked if they could hide until the chieftain was no longer looking for strangers.

Finally she agreed. "I will help you for your father's sake, Rima."

When darkness fell, the woman slipped away.

"I hope she does not turn us in," muttered Brill.

"She probably went to listen for news," said Rima.

In an hour, she returned. "They have not found the crown." She lowered her voice to a whisper, "Nadit, the smuggler, will help you over the wall when everyone is asleep. He owes me a favor."

In the middle of the night, the smuggler knocked softly on her door. Silently they followed him through the dark streets to his house beside the wall. From his flat roof they scrambled up onto the wall. He lowered a rope over the edge and held it as they climbed down the outside of the wall. Segra was the last one to go. "Thank you," she whispered.

"Do not mention my name if you get caught," he whispered back.

"We will not," she promised. "You have been very kind."

They crept away from the city, then circled back to the place where they had left their horses. They mounted and rode to the sea. A full moon lit the white surf as it crashed against the beach. Segra dismounted and entered the cave she had pointed out to Stargull. But it was too dark to see anything inside.

"We will have to wait until daylight," she said.

"The sooner we can get away from Khalom's territory, the safer we will be," exclaimed Rima.

"I will light a fire," said Brill. He gathered dried grass and some small pieces of driftwood. He struck sparks with his fire stones, and soon a small fire lit up the stone walls of the cave.

Segra looked around quickly. No jeweled crown caught the flickering light. "Where is Stargull, and what did he do with the crown?"

"He must have known it was not safe to land with all the soldiers looking for him," said Brill. He was searching the rocks at the back of the cave.

Rima, who stood watch at the entrance, whispered, "We must get on our way."

Brill scattered the burning embers with a stick, and they mounted their horses again.

For the rest of the night and all the next day, they rode hard, following the coast road. Segra kept looking up, wondering about Stargull. Had he been shot? Had she led him to his death?

They reached the capital by late afternoon. They found Vorn in the marketplace, selling his fish.

Lopet hugged Segra excitedly. "Where is the crown?"

"Stargull took it, but we do not know what happened to him," she said.

"Well, I am glad to see you back safe and sound," Vorn said. "But there is no room for horses on the boat."

"You are right," said Segra. "Rima, you may have the horses to sell or keep, whichever you want."

Rima looked at her with tears in her eyes. "Are you telling me to go away?"

"As I said before, you are free. I only wanted to save you from Omed."

"I do not want to leave you, Segra. Would you mind if I came with you?"

Segra smiled. "No, I would like that very much." She grasped Rima's hand. "You are a good friend. We never could have survived this adventure without you."

Rima smiled back. "I will always be grateful to you for rescuing me from Omed. I sometimes dream that I belong to Omed, and I wake up shivering."

"We are going far away from Asperita. You never need worry about Omed again." Segra squeezed Rima's hand and released it. "Let us go to the place where we bought the horses and sell them back."

When they returned to the fish market, Vorn was ready to leave. They boarded the fishing boat, and slept there overnight. The next morning a stiff wind pushed them north. Segra scanned the sky until her eyes watered. Surely, if Stargull were all right, he would look for her. She wanted to ask Vorn to make a detour to Pover to search for him, but Vorn was eager to get home. She could not ask for more favors.

In two days they were ready to cross the bay between Exitorn and Magra. The sea was calm. Vorn and Brill rowed while Segra and Rima watched for rocks. Lopet was ready to bail if the waves got too high.

They reached Molter on the afternoon of the third day. Vorn steered the boat into the harbor.

"Thank you, dear Vorn, for taking us to Asperita," said Segra. "We shall forever be in your debt."

"I wish you could have found the crown."

"You were a great help to us," said Segra. She hugged Lopet, and everyone said good-bye.

Later, as they walked along the winding city streets toward the palace, Segra said, "We have been gone for so long! What are my parents going to say?"

"And they will wonder about Rima," said Brill.

Segra bit her lip. "Oh—that is right. I will have to tell how I bought Rima. I will not lie. But let us not mention the crown. They would only worry."

As soon as Segra saw her father's face, she knew her parents were already worried. "You were gone much too long," said Prince Silgar.

"I imagined all sorts of terrible things," added her mother. "I only expected you to be gone a few days, but it has been almost two weeks."

Segra sat down beside her father. "We went to Asperita."

"Why would anyone go there?" he exclaimed.

"Vorn sold a lot of fish," said Brill.

Segra explained how she had rescued Rima, then asked, "Is King Gabron still as unreasonable as when we left?"

Prince Silgar nodded. "He has sent a letter to my father saying if he does not receive the crown or Velvet Valley in thirty days, I will be killed."

"Maybe he is only saying that to frighten Grandfather," Segra said hopefully.

"Perhaps he is, but I am worried that Father will decide to invade Asperita to find the crown," said her father. "I do not want soldiers killed to save me."

Tears of frustration filled Segra's eyes. If only we could have found the crown, Father would be safe, she thought.

The next morning Brill and Segra took Rima up to the tower. "This is our special place," explained Brill. "No one else comes here."

"It is a great view." Rima peered over the battlements. "Look at all the islands."

"If you look the other way, you can see mountains," said Brill.

Segra leaned against the stones. "We must think of some way to help Father."

Brill gave her a worried glance. "I cannot think of anything more that we can do. Surely King Gabron will not carry out his terrible threat."

"I do not trust him." Segra gazed at the green islands. Gulls flew back and forth over the fishing boats in the harbor. One of them, brilliant white, soared higher than the rest. Her heart beat faster. From here it looked small, but could it possibly be Stargull?

The bird circled, then turned toward the tower. She shaded her eyes against the sun's glare. It looked larger now, with huge, powerful wings that beat tirelessly toward her. Closer and closer it came. Silver-tipped feathers flashed in the sunlight.

"Stargull!" she cried. "Oh, Stargull, you are all right." The bird circled above the tower then glided to a landing on the low wall. Segra threw her arms around the sleek white neck.

The bird uttered a low squawk, deep within its throat. "He is trying to talk," Rima said. "It is too bad we cannot understand his language."

"Are you trying to tell me what happened?" asked Segra.

He squawked more loudly, cocking his head at her. Then he unfurled his giant wings and took off.

"Oh, do not go," cried Segra. She watched in disappointment as he flew back toward the islands.

"What do you suppose he was trying to say?" asked Brill.

"I do not know—unless he wants us to wait here." The bird grew smaller and smaller until it disappeared in the distance.

"Your parents will be expecting us for lunch," said Brill. "We could return later on."

Segra took one last glance at the harbor, then followed Brill and Rima down the narrow, winding stairs of the tower. "I am coming back right after lunch," she declared.

That afternoon the three returned to the tower. They all wore their cloaks this time, for a cold wind blew in from the sea. After a while, Brill took Rima on a tour of the castle and grounds, but Segra refused to leave the tower. She scanned the horizon and inspected each cloud until her neck felt stiff from looking up. The wind swirled past the tower, and she clutched her cloak tightly.

It was late afternoon when she saw the meladora bird approaching. Grasped in his talons was something that glinted in the sunlight.

She held her breath, afraid the vision would vanish. Closer, closer, he flew, until she was sure that he carried a circlet of dazzling brilliance. A minute later, Stargull swooped down to the stone wall and placed a very real crown at her feet. Tears of happiness misted her eyes as she hugged the bird.

"Oh, Stargull, you must have hidden the crown on Pover and waited for me to return to the castle." She picked it up, holding it close to her. "You knew this was the safest place to bring it. How can I ever thank you?"

He cocked his head as if satisfied. He stayed for a few minutes longer, preening his feathers while Segra talked softly to him. Then the great meladora bird spread his wings and sailed off on an updraft of wind.

Segra watched until he disappeared, then she crouched close to the tower to examine the crown. It had a cap of black velvet, like pictures she'd seen of old-fashioned crowns. The magnificent central diamond was flanked by emeralds, amethysts, and rubies. On each side was worked the pattern of a flying bird with emerald wings and an amethyst body, all outlined in diamonds. Perhaps it was meant to portray the ancient meladoras, she thought. And just think—a meladora bird had rescued it!

She tucked the crown under her cloak and hurried to her parents' room.

"Where is Father?" she cried.

"King Gabron has summoned him to the great hall." Her mother's worried expression changed to one of surprise. "What is it, child? What are you hiding?"

Segra opened her cloak. "The lost crown of Magra."

Her mother's eyes widened in astonishment. "Quickly—take it to your father. You may be just in time."

Segra ran down the stairs to the great hall. She heard King Gabron's loud, impatient voice. "To show him I mean business, you shall wait in a dungeon. I must have Velvet Valley! I have sent a messenger to King Talder to demand his final answer."

"My father will not give you the land," declared Prince Silgar.

"Then you will die," Gabron roared.

Segra held her cloak closed as she approached the throne, bowing to the king. "I would like to speak to my father," she said.

King Gabron looked outraged. "We are having an important discussion."

"Let me speak to my daughter," said Prince Silgar.

Segra turned her back on the king and pulled the jeweled crown from under her cloak. She handed it to her father.

Prince Silgar took it gently into his hands. "Where did you get this, my child?"

"From Asperita." She turned to the king. "You promised to release my father if the crown was returned."

Gabron leaned forward, staring in disbelief, and Prince Silgar put the crown in the king's outstretched hand.

He turned it over and over. Finally he found his voice. "The great diamond—and the jeweled birds. It is just as I remembered." Gabron placed the crown on his head, then removed it to admire the gems set in the sparkling rare metal.

"I will arrange for our departure at once," said Prince Silgar, taking Segra by the hand.

Gabron looked at Segra. "Did King Talder invade Asperita to get it?" he asked hopefully.

She shook her head. "No soldiers were involved."

"But it is not possible to steal this crown! It was too well guarded. I have sent men myself, but they have all been killed by Khalom. How could you get it?"

"That is my secret. You have the crown, and we are going home."

"No!" he shouted. His eyes glittered. "I will not let you go until I know how you got the crown."

Prince Silgar said, "You cannot ignore the promise you made before all the nobles of your court, King Gabron."

"But why will this daughter of yours not answer my question? I will keep her here until she tells me."

Segra did not dare to mention Stargull for fear Gabron would try to capture the bird. So she said quietly, "In the days to come you will hear many strange tales about the crown of Magra. Believe them if you wish, but I will tell you only that a friend of mine took it from Khalom."

Gabron glared at her. "How was this friend of yours able to do such a thing? It is not possible."

"But it happened, King Gabron." Segra stared right back at him. "Many Asperitans know that the crown did not belong to Khalom and that he is a cruel and dishonest man." She took a deep breath. "The Book of Wisdom says, *A dishonest man will meet disaster as surely as a moth flies into the flame.* Khalom met disaster, for without the crown, he may lose his throne. I trust that you will keep your promise, King Gabron."

King Gabron looked away. He lifted the crown and ran his fingers over its sparkling jewels. "No other king has such a beautiful crown. Every nobleman in the kingdom shall see it. We will plan a great festival of celebration." He smiled and added, "Surely, Prince Silgar, you will stay for the festival."

"My family and I must return home at once," Segra's father said firmly. He and Segra left the great hall. They returned to their rooms, and then Segra told her father and mother the whole story of how she had acquired the crown.

By the time Brill and Rima returned, servants had packed their belongings.

"We climbed the tower, but you were gone," Brill said.

"Stargull brought me the crown, and I returned it to King Gabron," answered Segra.

"We should have waited with you," said Rima. "I would like to have seen the crown close up."

"The important thing now is to get back to Exitorn," said Segra.

As they left their room, they saw that the guards were no longer outside their door. They hurried to the docks to book passage to Exitorn. "The sooner we get away from Magra, the happier I will be," Prince Silgar said.

"Do you think Gabron will change his mind?" asked his wife.

"Not for a few days, perhaps, but I do not trust him. When his joy over the crown fades, he may think of another scheme to get his hands on Velvet Valley."

Prince Silgar spoke to the captain of a ship that was sailing to Exitorn the next day. With an extra payment, they were allowed to stay in the captain's cabin overnight. They took turns watching the palace gates for any sign that King Gabron was sending his soldiers after them, but they saw no unusual activity.

The next morning when the tides were right, the ship sailed.

Segra, Brill, and Rima sat on deck and talked. "You will be my lady-in-waiting," Segra said to Rima.

"I would not mind being just your maid," she answered.

"Rima, if it had not been for you, we might still be in Asperita looking for that crown."

"I am going home to the farm," said Brill.

Segra answered, "I know that is what you want, but I will miss you."

When at last they were ushered into King Talder's throne room, the old man threw his arms around his long-lost son. "Silgar, you are home safe. My happiness is complete."

"It is wonderful to be home," said Prince Silgar. "And we have some wonderful tales to tell you."

King Talder put his arm around Segra's shoulders. "You who helped me escape from prison have now restored my son. And to think I did not know you were my own granddaughter!"

"My good friends, Brill and Rima, made it all possible," said Segra.

King Talder smiled. "Welcome to our castle, Rima." Then he turned to Brill. "I remember you well, Brill. Without you and Segra, I might never have recovered my throne. We will hold a great celebration and a parade to honor all of you. The people will rejoice to know that my son and his wife are home and that we have a brave little princess too."

"Segra has done enough brave deeds to last a lifetime," said Prince Silgar. "Now it is time for her to settle down to be a proper princess."

Segra wrinkled her nose. "Will that not be rather dull?"